BAROQUE-A-NOVA

KEVIN CHONG

G. P. Putnam's Sons
Publishers Since 1838
a member of Penguin Putnam Inc.
375 Hudson Street
New York, NY 10014

First American Edition 2002
Originally published by Penguin Books, Toronto, Canada

Library of Congress Cataloging-in-Publication Data

Chong, Kevin.
Baroque-a-nova / Kevin Chong.—1st American ed.
p.   cm.
ISBN 0-399-14825-6
1. Teenage boys—Fiction.   2. Indian youth—Fiction.   3. Women singers—Fiction.
4. Mothers—Death—Fiction.   5. Maternal deprivation—Fiction.
6. Suicide victims—Family relationships—Fiction.   I. Title.
PR9199.3.C4964 B3   2002   2001019543
813'.54—dc21

Printed in the United States of America
1   3   5   7   9   10   8   6   4   2

This book is printed on acid-free paper. ∞

Book design by Gretchen Achilles

THIS BOOK IS DEDICATED TO MY PARENTS.

THIS BOOK IS DEDICATED TO MY PARENTS.

There is no moment that exceeds in beauty that moment when one looks at a woman and finds that she is looking at you in the same way that you are looking at her. The moment in which she bestows that look that says, "Proceed with your evil plan, sumbitch."

DONALD BARTHELME, "The Sea of Hesitation"

BAROQUE-A-NOVA

MONDAY

Helena St. Pierre died one Monday. She was my estranged mother, a long-ago radio siren. I was eighteen, slack-jawed and gangly in army-surplus apparel, with narrow, miserly eyes and greasy hair falling in them, heavy and frizzy like wet yarn. I dressed like a badass, a surly malcontent: I wore sixteen-holed combat boots, dark jeans, and a dull green button-up shirt, a tiny East German flag patched to its right upper sleeve. Yet I couldn't grow a mustache if the fate of nations rested upon it. I was counting away the seconds of my last year of high school, of my last month, and while I didn't learn about it until later, I was at school, in class, staring at a ruler and sizing myself in millimeters, when she killed herself fifteen time zones away.

I was cranky. I came from a family of cranks; that was how I was made. I was the only native kid in school, half-blooded or otherwise, the only kid whose father had long hair and didn't hold a regular job, whose mother had run out under mysterious circumstances. We lived in a semirural area; this was not even a real suburb. I was used to getting the crap kicked out of me. It was right before lunch and I felt, then and there, an overwhelming sense of structure.

Theories had arisen to explain my apathy. My best friend, Navi, a young revolutionary, suspected I had fallen victim to the alienating effects of a market economy. My father would speak up from his recliner and say I was lazy. My stepmother would eye me nervously from the kitchen sink, thinking I might have a learning disability. My friend Rose said I was nihilistic. For a term in her AP lit class, she had read Russian novels: she quoted Maxim Gorky, who wrote in one of his suicide notes of a toothache in his heart.

They were all wrong. All I knew was that I felt adrift in longing, marshy and ungratified, in the smell of suntan lotion on freckled female shoulders. I felt dizzy with desire.

I was sad to the point of distraction.

Mr. Henry, our English teacher, had gone without coffee all day. He took stubby strides into class, and stifled a yawn as he wheeled a television and VCR to the front of the classroom, beside the yellowing poster of Knut Hamsun and a jade plant potted in a blue glazed vase. I was in English 12, where we were to be discussing a book I hadn't read because reading left so little time for important thoughts and activities. I had also lost my copy.

"Are we watching a movie?" I asked.

"Yes, Saul."

"I don't see any point."

"What are you getting at?"

"How does this film stimulate our critical-thinking abilities?"

"Right, I know how much you care about critical thinking."

Mr. Henry stepped back and looked at me, his chin swallowed by doughy flesh. He was in his forties, a not-so-tall round man with a mustache. He chewed toothpicks while marking papers and decorated his desk with model airplanes. I couldn't tell whether

Mr. Henry loathed me or liked me. He dealt with every student in the same offhand manner, with condescension and slight disapproval. And when he was bored with certain assigned texts, at certain times in the school year, he would allow certain loudmouth students to fill the class hour. I always stepped up, prompted by the very same tedium.

The class was silent; they waited for Mr. Henry to explode. The copies of our book, lugged here for no apparent reason, sat on their desks, their glossy paperback covers reflecting against fluorescent classroom lights. A book-banning felt so small-town, so feeble-minded, and it was only appropriate that my own school would so quickly pull it from our shelves, because no one wanted the trouble. I felt indignation welling inside me, struggling against my own natural apathy. Now I wished I had read the book, if only for the outrage it would have entitled me to.

"Have you given up on us already?" I asked.

"Some of you."

The class laughed. I raised my hand again.

"What about the book?"

"It's been pulled from the syllabus, Saul."

"Why?"

"Why? Because there have been complaints."

"Threats?"

"We don't want to take any chances."

"And how do you feel about that, Mr. Henry?"

"Hm. Well," Mr. Henry considered it, "not a whole lot. I would think you'd be one of the happier students, seeing the level of enthusiasm you've displayed for the assigned text over the past week. Have you even cracked it open?"

The room tittered. Some of my classmates—Mindy, the girl from the religious family who wore discarded nursing school slacks, and Tony, who had white scars across his wrists—rolled eyes, exchanged glances and pimply frowns, but they fell in the minority, among the scorned. A girl sitting in front of me, Nancy, the one with the big head of amber highlights, swiveled around and caught me with the corner of her eye, her mouth turned in a faint smile. I felt encouraged to go on.

"This is shit."

Mr. Henry yawned, cupping his mouth with a closed fist, his face catlike. "Please watch the language, Saul."

"Precisely. Language is the issue. Freedom of expression."

"All right, Saul, that's enough."

Usually a comment like this signaled an end to Mr. Henry's patience. With his amusement waning, we were to return to our studies, but I wasn't prepared to give it a rest.

"These days you need to resort to vulgarity to be heard," I said. "You have to bring the violence home. You're a child of the sixties: I'd think you'd understand."

He raised an eyebrow and leaned back against his desk.

"What are you saying?"

"If I were to call the school and make an obscene threat, maybe then people would listen."

Mr. Henry snickered. He turned off the lights in the room, casting our faces in the blue glow of the screen. Then he held up two cassette tapes.

"What will it be?" he asked. "*The Sweet Hereafter* or *The Handmaid's Tale*?"

"I hope you understand that I must leave this class in protest."

Mr. Henry sighed. He would have to report my absence, and I would end up in the principal's office again.

"Oh, Saul. Grow up."

I left class, found Rose in the library, and persuaded her to leave early. Rose couldn't say no to me. Fortunately, she was the only one who suffered from such a tragic affliction. Her parents worked during the day, so we went to her house, ate bite-size microwave pizzas in front of the TV, removed our clothes, and had maybe two and a half hot minutes of sex. Rose and I had had relations, as my stepmother liked to call it, for the first time a month before, shortly after she'd recovered from mono. We were in my dad's car by the beach, under a gray sleeping bag.

Rose stood now on the balls of her feet, flossing in front of her bathroom mirror. What can I say about Rose? She was about average height and wore her brown hair down to her shoulders. She had olive skin and incredible eyebrows. She was sweet-tempered and kind.

She was a dental-hygiene freak.

She flossed meticulously and exactly, each tooth a tiny precious stone. Flossing was a function of her obsessiveness, especially now that we had started "having a relationship." Lately, she'd been acting paranoid, guilty, as though we had stolen something valuable and tripped a silent alarm in our escape. Our conversations now involved hours of nagging. Nights of nagging. Nag-o-ramas. I started thinking of our arguments collectively as Nagtoberfest. First, I was roundly chastised for being withdrawn and sullen, for appearing at her house late at night, asking to be let in through the back door, and making her lie to her parents, who hated me. Then she said I was shallow. Me. We had been friends since sixth grade, but not once had I thought of her in a romantic way, not even one platonic kiss on her cheek, until she got sick and lost all that weight. She was putting it back on now, her face filling out and her belly showing, white, rippled, and squishy, and this was making her irritable.

Her mouth was twisted and drool ran down her chin. She noticed me and threw her floss into the wastebasket. Nagtime.

"I think we should reconsider our relationship," she said, wiping her chin with a tissue, then scrubbing her hands under the tap.

"What do you mean?"

"My parents know about us."

"No they don't."

"They do. They see you standing between me and the accredited postsecondary institution of my choice."

I paused, putting on a wounded expression. "Your parents should quit smoking crack," I sneered.

"My parents are not on crack." Rose suddenly sounded hurt.

Her parents were environmental rights lawyers who made sandwiches with pesto. Of course, I'm one to talk about weirdo parents, with such lunacy in my family. But at least my dad—for all his many, many faults—had a sense of humor. Rose certainly didn't, and now it seemed she might start crying, her eyes welling up the way milk rises to the brim of a glass and teeters there. In Science 10, we had learned a scientific word for that, and I sat on her bed trying to remember it.

Then I wondered how quickly I could make it home.

I got dressed and went to the kitchen. In spite of the pizza we'd just had, I felt hungry, like I could eat dog food if the situation got desperate, and began looking for something to gnaw on. I had excellent foraging skills, as I was always hungry and had access to strangers' kitchens. There were potato-and-onion pirogis in the freezer. I set about cooking them, scraping burnt chili from a pot in the sink and filling it with water. I put the pot on the stove, let the water heat, then added the pirogis.

Rose sat at the kitchen table.

I held up the bag of pirogis. She shook her head.

"I'm not hungry."

The pirogis started to float in the bubbling water. I normally liked them with fried onions, but I was too hungry for anything remotely ambitious. I drained them and put them on a plate; they were lumpy and white and wedge-shaped, like newborn strudels. One piece stuck to the bottom of the pot, so I pried it loose with a plastic spoon from the drain board.

"I should go to my dad's after I eat," I said. "The school has probably called him."

"Sure," Rose said. "Whatever you say."

I asked her where her parents kept the cutlery.

"Let me get it for you," she said, moving to a drawer. She cleared one half of the table, cluttered with newspapers and lawyer-type newsletters, and placed a knife and fork neatly in front of me. Then she stepped to the counter and watched me eat. There was a look on her face, a look I'd seen on my stepmother when she talked about my father, a stunned, heart-struck expression. So this is how you do it, I thought, stuffing pirogis into my mouth. Without trying.

She picked up the napkin dispenser from the counter and set it down straight in front of me, between us.

"Here," she said. "Talk to this."

My father had an entire house to himself, a one-story painted a thoughtful, nursery-school blue, with a flat roof and a carport, on a street lined with modest houses, bric-a-brac homes with gnomic statuary, and fussy latticed gardens. His house was on a cul-de-sac. After the last St. Pierres concert, Dad retired here in the older part of our town, a suburb on the West Coast. This was where I grew up, with him and my stepmother, Jana, the woman who had raised me since I was a four-year-old.

My parents had made up a musical duo, the St. Pierres, my mother the singer and my father the guitarist and principal songwriter. Their genius lay in flimsy balladry, schmaltz, and they found success in the seventies churning out folk rock, mid-tempo and sad, with occasional orchestral flourishes. They were like so many other singer-songwriters of that period, right before disco and punk crowded them off the airwaves. Until recently, none of my friends had even heard their music, its honky electric piano and treacly arrangements, those dated wah-wahs and synths on the last two albums. Then a German band named Urethra Franklin remade one of their songs into a top-forty hit, sampling the chorus to "Bushmills Threnody." I'd been hearing my mother's voice a lot in the past few weeks. People said she had run away—at least that was how my father put it. I pictured a woman floating down a river on a barge, a bundle-and-stick over her shoulder.

I wanted to run away, too.

Instead, I was living with my stepmother. In the past few months, visits to my father had come irregularly, usually when I wanted money or needed permission slips signed. According to the law, Dad was still my legal guardian. I was hoping to mention today's incident to him before the school called. What upset me was the thought that they might ask him to school and that he would fail to appear, as he had the last two times, not remembering the appointment or not caring enough to show. I figured I should have a word with him about fecklessness, about direction and responsibility.

I stepped through the front hallway, not bothering to take off my boots, and into the narrow kitchen. The sink window allowed a dusty light in the afternoon. The entire kitchen was under renovation: the cabinets gutted, the floors ripped up, a piece of tarp covering a hole in the ceiling. The month before, on one of the few sunny days that May, Dad talked about a glassed-in porch, a real yuppie add-on. I was surprised that though he eventually decided against the porch, he had decided to renovate the rest of the kitchen. It was something my stepmom had wanted done a couple of years back, when they were still together. "It's costing me ten thousand dollars," he would say. "Ten thousand dollars"— his avaricious refrain.

The living room was paneled, and included a fireplace. The carpet was thick and shaggy, patterned in a gray-black-blue marble swirl. A set of *World Book* encyclopedias and Dad's dubbed movie collection—all westerns—took up an entire wall. When Jana left, she'd stripped the place bare of its knickknacks, among them the commemorative plates that weren't for eating from and the colorful throws that had once covered the couches but now seemed out of place, unsettled like confused pets, on her new furniture. I expected to see Dad here, bare-chested in a pair of shorts, high or drunk, watching afternoon television—no doubt the cooking channel. I expected to see him scratching his stomach, his eyes bloodshot and narrow. I expected him to sigh when I walked in.

Instead there was a young woman, someone I didn't know, sitting on the couch where he should have been. She was in her twenties, a blonde with thin eyebrows, wearing a white tank top, pajama bottoms, and flip-flops.

"You're Saul, right?"

She offered her hand daintily, fingers scraping across my palm. Her name was Marina.

"I'm a friend of your dad's, I guess. From out of town."

"Since when?"

"Pretty recently."

"You're staying with him?"

"For a while," she said.

She flashed her bottom row of teeth. Then she looked toward the ground and began to bite her thumbnail. She was sitting on the black leather loveseat my stepmother had bought at a fancy secondhand shop in the city. It was placed between a banged-up recliner and a bentwood armchair. Her knees were in the air, and she looked pretty brilliant in a tank top—I tend to notice these things—her features finely cut and expressive. She seemed foreign, a woman with a story, like a Denny's hostess who was once a star of television and cinema in a former satellite country, a nation pocked with creaky nuclear reactors. I focused on her feet, her toenails painted green, and thought how perfect they were, her thin ankles held together as if by a loose, invisible knot. She looked good.

"How long are you visiting?" I asked.

She yawned, her head falling back on her shoulders.

"Don't know. Week, maybe two. I'm here with my friend Louise. She and I aren't on much of a schedule."

I was intrigued by the thought of two women.

"Where's Louise?"

"She's in the guest room."

"Where's my old man?"

"Ian's out for the afternoon running errands, filling the propane tank for the grill. He's having a barbecue tonight. You coming?"

I found the remote and turned on the TV.

"I guess."

"Shouldn't you be at school?" she asked.

"School sucks." I spat this out with as much nonchalance as I could manage.

She bobbed her head in a friendly, ingratiating fashion.

"I finished my degree in communications last May. Wrote my thesis on the female gaze in televised women's golf. I wouldn't recommend college. Though, I don't know, maybe you'll like it more. Your situation might be different. With me, it was all about normalizing."

"Normalizing?"

"Academia is the culture of normalization."

"Oh."

"You can say I've had enough school."

"How do you know my dad?"

"Louise and I wrote him a fan letter."

I sat down on Dad's squishy couch, stunned. From there, I picked up an issue of *Maclean's* from January 1994 on the coffee table, put it down, then tried to make sense of things. I wondered whether my dad had had his way with Marina. The thought didn't sit so well.

Another woman appeared by the kitchen entrance, carrying a laptop computer. Her face was the size of a hand and pretty, her eyes crinkled toward one another.

Marina introduced Louise.

"I'm making coffee," Louise said. She smiled nervously, placed her laptop on the coffee table, then disappeared into the kitchen. She had lovely arms. And she really did have a pretty face, although her hair looked as if it had been dyed one too many times; it was now the color of a cup of tea made from a reused bag.

"We corresponded," Marina said. "Three letters, one phone call. I sent him a photo, a picture of the two of us after we'd played tennis, you know, to show that we were sporty. We decided to travel this summer. Both of us had a little cash pocketed, so we came west. First we took one long train down to New Mexico and hung around with my mom and her, like, sixteenth husband. Two weeks ago we ended up on a bus to Portland, just five hours south, because we'd heard good things about it." Marina made a sour face. "We thought it would be fun to come up. Ian said he'd pick us up on Friday, at that town right before the border. What's it called—Blaine? Sounds about right."

Louise came back into the living room and sat next to Marina. She held a Scotiabank mug and started tapping away at her laptop. "You look puzzled, Saul," she said.

"I guess I am."

"Well, come on. Spill the beans."

"My dad's not rich, you know." This was true. My father blamed the government for the fact that he wasn't wealthy. There were layabouts, he complained, getting free chiropractic work and mammograms off his sweat. Still, for someone so concerned about money, he never worked. Mostly he puttered and drank. He phoned his lawyer to check whether any intellectual property had recently been stolen—no such luck. He went to the public library to send abusive e-mail to his stockbroker, whose advice he had taken on bad oil investments. "I mean, if you think he's rich, then you're completely off base."

Marina scanned the living room. "You don't say."

"Then what's the big deal about my old man?"

"Saul," Louise said, her eyes bulging, "your father's a fricking genius. There are these things on that album, little sounds that come out of the left speaker that you can't hear without a good set of headphones: Tibetan percussion, telephones ringing. He single-handedly revitalized the glockenspiel in pop music. No one used glockenspiels before your father. Now it's an industry standard.

Everyone focuses on Helena St. Pierre, on her voice—you know, conceptual artist, oppressed person, blah, blah, blah—but they don't really understand that Ian provided the substance in the band. His music is sensitive, yet masculine."

"His music," Marina said, "makes me feel among people."

Louise looked at her and nodded. "He's like the Toshiro Mifune of pop music."

We were watching the French-language music channel, which was exactly like the English-language music channel, only with pouty Québécois VJs who all seemed to be wearing clam-diggers. I wondered whether my father really was that famous, worthy of attention from strange young female admirers. Maybe it was Urethra Franklin that had brought their attention to my father. I had been watching the French-language channel the night before at Rose's when it aired an interview and a clip of the band performing their "Bushmills" cover, fast gaining popularity in North America. The keyboardist spoke about listening to smuggled St. Pierres records when he was growing up in Communist East Germany. He went on about my Indian mother, a woman who had disappeared from public view almost twenty years before, and about the beauty of the native people. Then there was another clip, from the coming-of-age gangster comedy that featured the song on its sound track.

Dad had griped only a month before about how little money he was getting from the group, compared with what they were making from his song. He said he intended to change lawyers over it. I supposed there were other benefits to be had from this renewed interest.

I gave Marina the eye.

"Any plans while you're here?" I asked.

"What do you have in mind?" she said.

"There's a water park down the highway. A ten-minute drive." I pointed out the window. "You can actually see it from the backyard."

"Is it much fun?"

"It's mostly for the under-twelve set, but bigger people are allowed."

"*Bigger* people."

"Whatever," I said, flustered. My face felt warm.

She smiled radiantly.

"Louise has your dad's biography, one written by a puffy-faced fellow. His face takes up the whole back cover."

"Erickson," Louise said. "I found it at a used-book store for twenty-five cents. It was in a barrel."

"I know people who work there," I said. "They have staff keg parties the last Thursday of the month—if you're going to be here that long."

"There's a picture of you in it on a sled, with you all tiny."

"*Adorable*," Marina said.

"Oh." I remembered the picture. "That must've been taken—probably at my grandparents'. They lived in North Ontario."

"You look like your dad," Marina said.

"Fine. No water slides."

"His eyes. Those gorgeous eyes."

I had his eyes, which were narrow and gray, and his Hungarian-count eyebrows, which flared out toward his temples. I had his bony hands and his rounded shoulders. I would probably inherit his stocky midsection. We walked the same way, sort of bow-legged and slouched, and we sounded alike when we answered the phone—groggy and impatient and needy all at the same time, an emotional boilermaker. I wondered when this had taken place, under my nose, how I'd turned into my father. It must have happened in my sleep.

"But you have your mother's coloring. Her Native American cheekbones."

"So you're here you don't know how long?"

"Precisely," Marina said.

I went home to Jana's, taking the pedestrian overpass that stretched above the highway. We lived in a flat, drained municipality thirty minutes south of Vancouver whose outskirts were populated by faded barns and electrical towers. It was early in June. The weather was warm and clear, breezy, a welcome change from April and early May, when it had been gray and wet. From the overpass I could see traffic wash in from the city along Highway 17 past the intersection, the hockey and curling rinks, the cow pastures where new housing developments were planned, the highway leading toward Tsawwassen and the ferry to Vancouver Island. We were right by the ocean. I stood over rumbling cars at the intersection: sedans pulling motorboats, green Celicas and blue Accords driven by men in suits—sunglasses installed on their prescription eyewear, and parking stubs collecting on their dashboards—trucks with cabs, a Volkswagen Passat with two women in saris, a BMW with a body board on its roof, a junky Datsun rusted the color of a nosebleed.

Drivers could read about Marcel and Ivy's twentieth anniversary. Or the hockey team. People hung signs from the Day-Glo-green overpass railing, bedsheets spray-painted with endearments. Up ahead, the highway was being repaved. I saw a woman in an orange vest directing drivers to one lane.

Two fire engines crossed Highway 17 into town, their sirens ornery, followed by a pair of police cars.

An old Chinese woman sat at the bus stop in a floppy garden hat, her feet not touching the ground.

Here trees stood tall and narrow, planted in rows to prevent soil erosion.

I spat on a Chevy Nova.

The farther east you went, the newer the houses were. Navi lived in the development beside the overpass, a giant gray house with darker gray trim that fit at least thirteen people and a Steinway played by his brother, an eleven-year-old prodigy, among other boxy houses in cul-de-sacs. My stepmother's townhouse was just beyond. These homes had appeared only in the past ten years or so. I remembered playing baseball past where Navi lived, back when it was an empty lot, but now the area was overrun with homes, housing mostly Indian families. Sikhs. Men with turbans and beards. Women who traveled in pairs, in gold-flecked orange, beet, and yellow fabrics. They kept their lawns trim and undecorated. They took up about two-thirds of the high school. An Indian veteran had not been allowed to enter the local legion hall on Remembrance Day because he was wearing a turban, and headwear was forbidden. The story had gotten into the newspapers, and our homely little suburb was declared the hate capital of the province.

I leaned forward against the railing, as far as I could stomach, until I was almost horizontal. I watched the old woman at the bus stop watch me, disapproving, then finally uninterested.

I wanted to leave.

The landscape, the flatness, the low-slung buildings.

I spat on a blue Honda Civic.

My stepmother was dressed to go out, in a satin blouse with a string of pearls around her neck, as she carried a basket of dirty laundry to the closet facing the stairs, where the washer-dryer was located. We lived in a townhouse complex, a collection of narrow salmon-colored buildings encircling a parking lot and the grassy, shrubbed median at its center like a bull's-eye. The development was quiet, especially during the day. Its residents were either retirees and divorcées like Jana, who worked as an office temp, or young professional couples, accountants and lawyers intent on owning a home—people on their way up, or on their way down. There weren't any children here. No one, it seemed, went to the trouble.

"You're supposed to be at the principal's office at quarter to nine," Jana said.

A school secretary had phoned.

"Since when does the school call *you*?" I asked.

"Your father referred them to me after your last final warning." Jana shrugged, then placed the basket on the dryer and pulled out the whites from the rest of the clothes. "He says he hardly sees you, anyway."

"I bet he's crying buckets."

"Where were you today, if you don't mind me asking?" This was the way she asked questions—casually and off the beat.

I mentioned Rose and Dad, but left out his two visitors.

"How is Rose?"

"Studying, as usual."

"And is she feeling better? She's gotten so thin."

"She's getting heavier," I said.

"Oh. Well, that's good."

"She's turning into a whale."

"*Saul*, that's not nice."

Jana dumped towels and underwear into the washer, doused them with a capful of blue liquid, and closed the machine's lid. I grunted, then went to the kitchen.

Jana was from Cape Breton. She was short. She had thick hips and round cartoon eyes and was the most important person in my life. She followed me into the kitchen, where I found a cold cinnamon roll in the refrigerator and gobbled it down even though it was stale. I raised my eyes from the roll and looked at her. She seemed tired, her eyes puffy. She approached, placed a hand on my hip, and brushed my nose with her finger.

"You eat too much. Someday you'll have to pay for it. You'll pay through the nose."

"I'll find union work," I said. "I'm young, I'm eager. I'll go into forestry."

"I'm glad you have your life all mapped out."

"Oh, you know"—I smiled, and swatted my hand at her playfully—"I had a couple of hours free last night."

"And your father? How is he?"

"Same old, I guess."

"Hm. Same old something."

"He's renovating the kitchen."

"Well, la-di-da."

"La-di-da," I repeated.

"I have a date tonight."

"Officer Dale?"

"Mm-hm. We're going to sing karaoke at the Silver and Gold."

You're so lame, I thought, feeling shame surge across my face. Out of guilt, I offered to vacuum the house.

"As you may recall, I did that yesterday. But thank you, thank you for your hollow and, no doubt, limited-time offer." She went into the bathroom to put on earrings, walking the mannish way she did when hurrying, shoulders forward, hands in fists. "I'd appreciate it if you could fix your own dinner," she said from the doorway.

"I'm going to Dad's."

"Since when does he have you over for dinner?"

"Since now, I suppose."

Jana grunted like she was amused, but really she wasn't.

"Well, isn't he one for surprises."

She stepped out of the bathroom, clicking off the light, then found her purse on the kitchen counter, took out a pack of cigarettes, and lit one.

"Dale better not be late tonight. I swear."

My father had been a chain-smoker until he stopped cold turkey the year before, just to see if he could. Dad could do things like that. He thought it silly that others couldn't break habits as easily. He called it self-discipline—I sort of thought it a result of being such a hopeless strap-on. Jana had no such willpower. Even though she'd once told me that she smoked only because of being around Dad and she'd quit now that they were separated, there she was, puffing away.

I went upstairs to my room and lay on my bed reading comics, before turning on the radio. First the top-forty station and then the college station played "Bushmills Threnody," the German remix, which featured electronic dance sounds, spacy pulses, and my mother's sampled voice, over which the lead singer of Urethra Franklin rapped in brutal, politicized English.

The phone rang. Rose wanted to know whether I had heard about the toxic nerve gas.

"What?"

Somebody had called in a threat at school. Students were moved out, gathered on the soccer field, where they milled around nervously, discussing what was the year of *Anschluss*, movie adaptation versus comic book versus video game. They talked about *Star Wars* and Spice Girls and the chicks at school with the fattest asses. They sat on the grass and watched a couple of guys try to hacky-sack a green apple. A lonely girl sat alone with her guitar, strumming listlessly.

They watched the dumpster being searched. Policemen stood around. Experts, presumably, were consulted.

I figured some kid didn't want to write a chemistry exam. I thought it was funny, but Rose insisted it was no joke.

"It was on the news at six. Didn't you see it?"

Rose's family would eat dinner together with the news on. They would then retire to the living room, whereupon they would hold forth, like a panel discussion group, on the greater world at hand, a topic that led to endless discomfort for me whenever I was invited for dinner.

The door slammed downstairs. From the window in my room, I watched Jana step into Officer Dale's truck in the early-evening light. He was holding the car door, and her shoulders bent in deference to him, bearing the weight of his shadow. Officer Dale had a fire hydrant for a neck, a face all pink and sweaty, and an open yard of crew-cut blond hair. As a way of gaining my approval, he'd once let me try out his handcuffs, so I thought he was cool enough, even if he was a cop and his verbal skills weren't too astounding. Jana liked him, I could tell, because of the way she glanced at him, quickly, as if he were something that must be taken sparingly.

"You should really keep abreast of current events, Saul."

"I don't get the news."

There was a truck in Dad's driveway next to his Volkswagen Jetta, a truck belonging to his friend Gord. Gord owned a contracting business. Painted on the side of his truck was the company's logo—a cartoon caricature of a lanky hippie guy, docile and ingratiating, with nails in his mouth, swinging a hammer in the air. I slipped the latch and opened the back-fence gate. Even for the yards in this neighborhood, my father's was large, with yellow patchy grass—a neighbor's dog was always sneaking in through a hole in the fence to pee—and an unpainted picnic table. At the very end, beside a small fir tree, was a white toolshed where he kept a manual lawn mower. Past it, empty fields, then the highway. Dad was at the grill, Marina and the Coburns, Gord and Nadine at the picnic table. Louise sat on a stool next to Dad.

Stuck to the side of the barbecue was a blob of green plastic and bristle—a brush that had been left too close to the grill and melted on it like a squashed caterpillar. Dad stood looking over a set of pork ribs and some chicken wings. He took my hand and pulled me toward him, swinging his other arm, one with a pair of kitchen tongs, over my shoulder loosely in an awkward embrace.

"Why haven't you called?" he asked, returning to the ribs.

"I didn't know I was supposed to."

"I haven't seen you in weeks."

"Keeping busy."

"Oh, well. Good."

We didn't have much to say, never had.

Dad wiped his eyes, using his wrists.

"Don't these look good?" He nodded at the ribs.

"As usual."

"We'll eat well."

His tangly Summer of Love hair had been let down and fell to his shoulders, and he had shaved off his beard, which he'd worn carelessly for the past two or three months. He seemed healthier than the last time I had seen him, his belly stretching against a faded blue T-shirt. His legs were still pale and pasty in those camouflage shorts he had found at an army-surplus sale I took him to, but there was a smile on his round face, his eyes, my eyes, squinting and gleaming. Good for him, I thought.

Gord had chicken wings in his mouth. He had been Dad's pedal-steel player, the longest-serving member of the St. Pierres' touring band, and was Jana's old boyfriend. He was an inveterate pot smoker, six feet, six inches tall, in jeans and a Winnipeg Jets jersey, with a long face and white hair that ran down his back. After the band's demise, he started his own contracting business, doing small construction jobs and renovations, which now included Dad's kitchen. "Ten thousand dollars," Gord once huffed when Ian complained. "He doesn't know how cheap he's getting it." Nadine was his wife, maybe only a few years older than Dad's visitors. She was heavily made up, in hot pants and a belly shirt, her hair held back with a banana clip. She reminded me of a hamster. Her eyes were small and dark, and when you looked directly at her, her nose wrinkled.

Marina was still wearing her flip-flops. Gold-rimmed aviator specs sat atop her head in the accessorizing way women wear sunglasses. She was drinking sangria from a green plastic jug with a wooden spoon in it. She raised her face when she saw me approach, her eyes alighting on me slowly, and smiled on recognition. I sat down next to her.

"Let me pour you a glass, okay?" she said.

She took a plastic cup and filled it halfway and then scooped in pieces of fruit. It tasted strong, heavy on sherry, and a little vinegary.

Louise was talking. She wasn't really American, she was saying, but from Toronto, and working toward an international affairs degree at Columbia University.

"The international affairs is really a fallback." She smiled apologetically.

"Louise is working on a screenplay," Marina explained. "But now she's hit a rut."

"The problem lies in the second act. You come up with a great idea, great characters, great situations. And you know how you want to end it. Character X finds true love, then dies. But between all that you need so much relevant action."

"Louise is writing a feminist tragedy that might possibly include figure skating," Marina said. "Sparkling dialogue. Arresting social themes touched."

"You need to cook up subplots, leitmotifs that are rich in association. Thread them together."

"Louise is hard on herself. We're working on that."

"It's not as easy as it might sound. All the narrative strands don't exactly meet at the end."

"It was going to be a novel, but she's come to realize where her strength lies—in imagery."

"It's loosely based on the life of Margaret Trudeau Kemper," Louise said glumly. "Possibly with figure skating."

"It's not as stupid as she makes it out to be."

"How did the two of you get the summer off to travel?" Gord asked.

"Well," Louise said, "as I was telling Ian, our sublet expired in May. We had a deal on the place, a two-bedroom with a view. A French architect uses it in the summer—Henri, who designs airport terminals—and lets it out to young women as his way of supporting his labor-friendly ideals. We met him once."

Marina laughed through her nose. "He walked in unannounced," she said, "get this, wearing dark glasses and a black skullcap, like a longshoreman. He said work had let out two weeks early for him and that we all had to make like good friends. The story goes, he always surprises his female subletters. He walks around the house in Speedos. A forty-five-year-old lech who listens to hip-hop, who brought out a camera and said if we posed nude for him we could *reclaim* pornography. A real zeitgeist-monger, he is."

"You're the one who slept with him," Louise said. "May I add?"

"Okay, so what? There was nothing good on TV. The point remains."

"And he propositioned me, too."

Marina rolled her eyes. "The point remains that we have the summer free. Louise doesn't have to be back at school until September, and I quit my job at a discount mattress warehouse. We wanted to travel, do something with a goal, a cultural thrust. We made it our mission to hang out with people we admire. We wrote a fan letter, the literary form of the new century. We put our heads together, five glasses of wine into the night, and Louise typed the letter. About the St. Pierres, how *Bushmills Threnody*, that entire album, is, like, wicked awesome."

"We wrote other people, too," Louise said shyly, "but your dad was the only one who wrote us back."

"Kurt Vonnegut never wrote back. Peter Bogdanovich, neither."

"Well," Gord concluded, "it's good having you here." He pointed to the boombox on the table next to the Caesar salad, a sour, appraising look on his face, and turned to my dad: "What are we listening to?"

"The Rolling Stones. *Aftermath*. I just bought it on CD."

"Maybe that's the problem." Gord's face was still and thoughtful. "CDs sound cleaner, but there's something missing."

"It's scientific fact that digital technology, the encoding process," Louise said, "is reductive. It takes nuance and texture in sound and turns them into ones and zeroes. It amounts to sonic fascism."

Gord nodded along. "These days everything is political."

"Even the scratches, eh, Gord?" Nadine added, her mouth square and mocking.

"It's a warmer sound."

"Well, I guess I've missed the *sound*, since I've only listened to CDs. I've missed the *sound*." Nadine laughed scornfully. She always had to say something, be it about bad drivers or How the Medication Makes Me Feel or the *sound*. "You people take everything that's old and crappy and call it an antique. Or retro. You give it another name, and something bad is good. It's so—so ridiculous. Some things are good and some things are icky."

"Can we eat peacefully this one night?" Dad said from the grill, his voice high and scolding. He placed a hand to his chest and raised his tongs to the sky, then lowered his voice. "Friends and neighbors, let us lay down our arms and sup."

"Ridiculous," Nadine felt compelled to add.

"Your dad baked a carrot cake," Marina said.

"I didn't know he baked."

"I did the corn and the potatoes. Louise tossed the salad," Marina continued. Then she whispered into my ear, giggling, "Louise likes your dad. Pass it on."

I watched them. Louise took occasional nips of Dad's beer, looking like a girl in fifth grade as she sat on her stool, her chest thrust forward, her feet resting on the stool's rung. I thought she was pretty stuck-up. It seemed as though she was waiting for someone to pronounce her the smartest and the prettiest, the only one who knew how to French inhale. She resembled a bird, her tiny head bobbing back and forth on her shoulders. She was fawning at my father. She kept touching him, his elbow, the small of his back. Dad smiled, his face newborn-pink from alcohol as he sat down to eat. I almost remembered when I used to like him in spite of all his crap, when he could make an entire room quake with laughter.

The Caesar was a little oily, but I preferred oily to dry, and the corncob prunish-looking but sweet. The meat was greasy and tangy, a little smoky.

"Louise," Marina said, "I thought you were a vegetarian."

Louise held a pork rib with her thumbs and forefingers, as one would a harmonica.

"I know, I know. I've fallen off the wagon."

We sat and ate quietly. The CD ended, and Dad set the stereo to the CBC, which was playing something West African. We watched him disappear into the house, Louise on his trail in a white sleeveless dress, her shoulders sagging.

Past the yard, past the fields beyond, cars coursed along the highway, their lights on in the dusk. The sky, from the horizon up, was orange, then pink, then a bloody, wet purple. The noise of traffic in the distance was soothing, the buzz of passing cars meshing with the bug zapper, which hummed by the screen door.

Nadine stood up, went to the boombox and tuned the radio to a top-forty station that was playing a Mariah Carey song, then raised the volume. She took a seat on Gord's lap and twirled his thinning white hair in her fingers as she mouthed the lyrics. They began whispering to each other and nuzzling. I liked Gord, but couldn't figure how he could suffer someone as mindless as Nadine. There were some things I didn't understand. My heart fell for a moment.

Marina smiled at me, her eyes heavy. She opened her mouth to say something but seemed to forget what was on her mind. Her mouth hung half open and her bottom lip was wet. I decided then that my life would be a crushing defeat if I didn't at least stick my tongue down her throat in a private setting, somewhere dark. But I was just a young man, my hair goofy, my methods of seduction unproven, and my ludicrous father didn't make things any easier.

"How long has Dad been drinking today?" I asked Marina.

"Since the afternoon. He seems in pretty good shape, actually."

"Dad holds it pretty well until he starts throwing punches. What's the deal with him and Louise?"

"I went to bed early, so I can't say."

I mulled this over silently.

Then she added, almost purring, "You know, it was really her idea to come up here, more her idea than mine. I like the St. Pierres and all, but not as much as her. She was, like, wicked jealous about the French architect. She had a crush on the disgusting lech."

Dad and Louise emerged from the house reeking of weed, their faces red and guilty-looking. Louise's bra was showing. She carried out a half-eaten carrot cake in an aluminum dish.

"We sort of jumped the gun," she said.

Marina smiled, arching one eyebrow at me.

Dad held a big serving knife in one hand. He acted like the mother at a birthday party, a prissy, pretend schoolmarm, cutting little squares of carrot cake for us all. He took our plates and served the cake.

His eyes, bloodshot and blinking, landed on me.

"Saul," Dad said, "how was school?"

"Oh, you know. Business as usual."

A stupid smile spread over his face. Marijuana made him happy.

"I think you've turned into a fine young man, and I feel lucky that I didn't bugger that job."

"Thanks."

"Seventeen years old."

"Eighteen."

Dad turned to Gord, coughing into his armpit. "Take a look at him. Saul's eighteen, almost finished school."

Gord laughed. "Yeah, he's a big boy."

The radio station faded from the Mariah Carey tune to Urethra Franklin's "Bushmills Threnody."

Dad's eyes narrowed, and his chin buried into his chest. He seemed upset, then shrugged his shoulders and smiled. He pulled a lawn chair over to the picnic table and sat down.

"It's certainly catchy," he said. "I'll give them that."

"Urethra Franklin is like the Puff Daddy of Germany," Louise said. "This might well prove to be their crossover hit on this side of the Atlantic."

I sat picking at the crappy cake. The group's vocalist was rapping, his vocals megaphone-distorted and then electronically lowered in pitch.

"I can't really make out what he's singing," Louise said.

At this moment in history, the remade "Bushmills" belonged to a popular genre of music, wherein people sampled music, retooling and splicing it to fit their own dance beats. Old songs were given new life. And if the members of Urethra Franklin were supposed to have a social conscience in this political world, it was all that much better. In their politicized worldview, my mother was cast as the voice of its ravaged indigenous populations.

"Is that English?" Nadine asked.

"Poverty ice cream," I suggested.

"Properly crimes," Marina said.

"Sounds like garbage to me," Gord grumbled.

"The song's supposed to be about native rights, unfair land treaties," Louise said. "Property is a crime."

"Whatever happened to melody? To good feelings? The energy here is way off."

"He's probably singing phonetically," Marina said.

The rapping stopped for a measure, and then my mother's voice kicked in with the chorus:

> *I try to forget about you*
> *But you write, you telephone too*
> *Oh, my dear,*
> *Your hands so soft*
> *How can I sleep you off*
> *Like a hangover from the night before?*

"I was thinking Tom Waits when I wrote this, early Tom Waits," Dad said. "Or the Moody Blues. It was supposed to feature a string section. Imagine a string section and an even slower tempo. Thankfully Leni sang the way she did—we had to change the song to suit her—and it sounds nothing like the Moody Blues."

"Did you know I was in an art rock band in college?" Louise said, turning to Marina. "We were called the Children of the Corn. I played kazoo."

"It wasn't supposed to be a single. The record company wanted the song as a B-side, but a disc jockey in Philadelphia who had an advance copy liked 'Bushmills' better. New singles had to be pressed soon afterwards."

"What was it?" Louise asked. "What was the A-side?"

"'Kelvin Technical Blues,'" Dad said.

Not all mothers were like mine. Jana said my mother had run off to be with an old lover. Helena St. Pierre hated touring, the whole rotten business. Jana was on the last St. Pierres tour. The first time she met my mother, the frail and thin native woman with swollen and sunken Third World eyes, was backstage after a concert. Helena St. Pierre was sitting in a metal folding chair. It was strange, Jana thought, how everyone was ignoring her: the rhythm section eating cold cuts by the deli table next to her, the opening band griping about the sound check. My mother, dark and small. The truth was, she scared everyone on the tour. They were afraid to look her in the eyes, which at that moment were fixed on Jana.

"Am I in your chair?" she'd asked. Her voice was huskier than Jana had thought it would be; she spoke slowly and tentatively. "Do you want it?"

Helena St. Pierre with a voice honey-tinged and full-bodied, lead-heavy.

Helena St. Pierre, a famous singer with a domineering husband and a big case of stage fright.

Helena St. Pierre, who hated being famous.

Helena St. Pierre, who became unhinged, who abandoned her husband and her newborn son to shack up with an old boyfriend.

While we spoke at my father's picnic table, the sky was turning the same weepy blue as the house. I could hear the crickets chirping against the radio's static. There was a sliver of silence as the song faded out, and then the disc jockey identified the last song, artist and title, before mentioning that only hours before, my mother had thrown herself out of an apartment window in Thailand.

Inside the house, the phone was ringing.

Every story retold carries a measure of vengeance. I lived in a world of voices, each one calling out for blood. I knew my mother only by hers. I heard Helena St. Pierre on the radio, making her comeback, voluntary or otherwise. When I heard my mother sing, I wondered what score she had to settle.

TUESDAY

Jana drove me to school the next morning. Her car smelled like stale french fries, from too much drive-thru, our shared vice. Fries were jammed between the car seats and the hand brake, ketchup packets littered the ashtray. This was how a mother should smell—like fabric softener, like apple-scented conditioner and nail polish, like french fries.

She stopped the car near the school grounds. She ran a finger down my nose and *tsk*ed, then let me out behind a burgundy Volvo.

A clock by the cafeteria entrance read eight fifty-five. I turned left along the corridor leading to Administration, ran my knuckles against the lockers. My boots squawked on the floor.

The school kept a trophy cabinet beside the office, and portraits of the queen and the prime minister. The secretary waved me through, as if truancy were hanging over me like a tarnished halo.

In his office, the principal, Mr. Choi, leaned back in his chair and laughed on the phone. Another man stood beside him, resting a hand on top of a file cabinet.

Officer Dale pointed to a chair opposite Mr. Choi.

He stepped across the room, keys jangling on his belt; he moved with a loud bounce, like a piano shoved over a speed bump.

He went through his questions and scribbled my information in his black-vinyl–covered notepad. Mr. Choi finished speaking on the phone. He looked sour and still. His hair was heavily greased, and there were patches of gray above his temples. I told Dale where I had been the day before.

He sucked in his gut and let it roll out.

"I didn't do anything," I said.

"That's all I wanted to hear, Saul. I honestly didn't think . . ."

And so I stood to go. The principal put down the phone as I reached the door.

"All done, are we?" he asked Dale. His face widened, and the lines around his mouth creased disagreeably, bellowing like a hand organ. Mr. Choi was a weaselly autocrat who handed out suspensions to kids caught smoking. One girl found drunk at a school dance—the one who had "problems at home"—was expelled. "The boy has a history of troublemaking. He made a threat yesterday in his English class."

"What about it?" I sneered back. "I didn't do a fucking thing."

"Listen to him. Just listen."

Dale ignored him, and nudged his head toward the hallway. "I need to give a message to the boy's stepmother."

Dale followed me into the hallway, then waited until a girl, an eleventh-grader in bicycle shorts, passed us.

I slumped back against the lockers. I felt like heaving. That morning I'd had half a slice of dry toast and two extra-strength Tylenol for breakfast and chased it down with flat Pepsi from a two-liter bottle in the refrigerator.

"Son, I want you to know we can talk," Dale said. "That I take off this uniform when we speak."

I must have smirked.

"You know what I mean."

"I'm all right."

Dale put his hand on my shoulder, his thumb brushing against my neck, and nodded solemnly. He smiled shyly, and his face reddened. I wondered how he had learned to be such a great communicator, whether he had taken classes on sympathy at police school, or if there were professional days devoted to the subject. We were both possessed with shame.

"Some crackpot phoned in this nerve gas business, complaining about a book that's being taught here, and the people here are looking for students to blame. That was just ridiculous, that interview." He hooked a finger in the loop of his belt. "Saul, you're a good kid, a real good piece of work—everything considered."

"Thanks."

"This may sound bad. He's still your father and you've got to give him that." He paused. "But I hear things about him from Jana. We were talking about you just yesterday."

"How was karaoke night?"

"It's on Wednesday. This is really crazy, this situation. Not karaoke night, but this toxic nerve gas situation. Because it didn't make anyone in this community look like hot poopoo. Everyone thinks we're backward here as it is, because of the whole turban incident."

Dale put a hand on his belt and hiked it up and down. His face was still red and he smiled crookedly, his eyes fixed on his nose.

"If I thought you were someone who was worth suspecting, I wouldn't be telling you, as I'm doing now, about the locker search at noon."

After my heart-to-heart with Dale, I ran into the washroom. At the sink I threw up, spewing out what looked like rancid spumoni. Then I wiped my face with brown paper towels that I had clumped into tragic little balls. I found a toilet stall with a latch. Snot skidded down my nose, and I coughed until my face was wet with tears.

I remained on my knees, elbows against the toilet bowl. There were two people using the urinals. One of the fluorescent tubes buzzed on and off, making a rattling sound. The light coated the washroom in a gray glaze. For a while I didn't do anything; I didn't move.

Then I ran brown toilet paper along my eyes and threw up again.

Say you never knew your mother. Say she was some crazy native woman, a manic-depressive who went off, disappeared, when you were an infant. She left to be with another man. And your father shuts up whenever her name is mentioned. Say that everything you know about your parents you find in a paperback biography. Say that your mother's death leaves you a little confused. Because the only other dead people you knew are your grandparents, who died a week apart from each other when you were twelve. You miss them but can't remember exactly what they looked like, and now you think of them as you do the Magna Carta, like dates and names.

Say your mother was an absolute nutbar and she killed herself because she hated hearing her voice on the radio.

Where was Thailand? Where the hell was it? Next to China, south of Korea, straddling the coast of whatever, drained by the river who cares, bounded by the hills of doesn't matter.

Underneath palm fronds and the tropical sun. She lived in Thailand, singing in a choir, teaching children to read, pleading with villagers not to sell their daughters. She lived by herself in an apartment complex near the church because only the priests and the nuns lived in the parish residence. Though she deemed herself impure for the job, she kept her room the way she thought a novice's cell should appear: a single bed, the Bible on the nightstand next to an analog radio alarm clock, on the wall a picture of Christ, shrink-wrapped in smoky plastic. She stayed on an almost liquid diet. Rice porridge and boiled cabbage. She was having back trouble. She placed a board under the mattress she slept on. She mended her old dresses, wore polyester slacks twice torn, and secretly prayed to God that no one would recognize her there, as far east as she could get. She couldn't help thinking about her husband, her son, hoping they had forgotten her.

Where was Thailand?

Where my mother was.

No place at all.

The bell had just sounded. I stepped into the hall, where other students were spilling out. A girl with red hair, a ninth-grader, tapped my shoulder. She was wearing a spaghetti-strap top over a red bra. These days women were dressing sexier at a younger age. Hootchie. They showed skin and they jiggled when they walked or line-danced or shot-putted. I couldn't help myself around them.

She wanted my autograph.

"You're really him, right? I rollerbladed to your parents' song last week."

I wrote my name in the lined notes section of her school agenda, a spiral-bound booklet with school holidays and attendance rules listed in the front and dated pages to keep track of homework assignments.

"Whom should I make this out to?" I asked. And I thought how silly that sounded coming from me. Whom should I make this out to.

She took back her agenda, stared at the page, and then pressed it against her chest. She started away, but pivoted around to face me.

"Hey, I just want to say, you know, sorry about your mom."

She hurried off, almost skipping, an invisible hand pushing her forward along the polished coffee-colored floors into second period.

This was how news traveled. The evening before, right after we'd heard about Helena St. Pierre's death, we moved inside silently, our feet swishing through the backyard lawn, heels scuffing against the bare kitchen floor as we entered the house. Dad had slipped in first through the sliding screen door to answer the phone. Gord and Nadine went home. Marina foraged in the refrigerator and found a bottle of vodka in the freezer and some soda water at the back of the vegetable crisper.

Louise put a stack of dishes in the sink. Her wrists were straw-thin, her cheeks rosy, her nose upturned. I could see how Dad would go for her. It was her meek nature. She was like a water-logged pastry, staring at me with her lips pursed, looking sort of frantic, as though she'd lost her passport or some other vital possession. Louise was about as small as my mother. Dad would like that. He hunched up his shoulders, he watched you, his reading glasses sliding down his nose, like a scavenger.

"You poor thing," she said.

I turned my back to her and glared. I began to follow Marina out of the room.

"Do you think it's a good idea for him to continue drinking?" Louise said, her voice a stage whisper. She opened the door under the sink and scraped bones from plates into the trash with a fork. "I'm worried about him."

"Don't let it . . ." I trailed off drunkenly.

"Don't let it what?"

"Don't let it keep you up at night."

In the living room, Marina sat on the couch, feet on the hassock. Her hands were folded on her lap, curled around a scotch tumbler. I dimmed the lights.

Marina's eyes closed as she yawned. "This is what I call a shit situation, Saul. A wicked shit situation."

"Don't look at me like that. Please."

She asked me what I meant.

"I hardly knew my mother, you know. It's no big deal."

She nodded. I sat down beside her on the black leather couch, which wheezed as I sank into it.

"We can talk about normal things."

I sat there watching her.

Marina smiled, then bit her lip.

"Don't you have a girlfriend?"

"Um, not really."

My head fell against my chest. I stared meaningfully at my shoes, morosely. I didn't have sufficient room in my heart for words. I was like my father, my miserable, sullen old man. Dad was a man of action, of cruel little gestures. He made me feel stupid not through putdown or criticism or even misplaced laughter, but simply by getting up for ice when I had anything to say.

I was like my father right now, sticking my hand up Marina's shirt.

Marina laughed as though she had been tickled. But her mouth stayed closed, and she gently pried herself away from me.

I brought my face up to hers. I felt her breath on me. She had wonderful breath. I sat back.

"Sorry," I said.

"Don't worry about it."

I could hear water running in the kitchen. Louise was doing the dishes. I was mad at her for being so stuck-up, for adoring my father and fucking around with him now, when he had more important things to deal with. I blurted out, "I hate her."

Marina took a sip from her tumbler and swallowed. "She's insecure."

"But she's so wonderful."

"She doesn't think anyone loves her."

"Well, so do I."

I took some vodka from the bottle sitting on the coffee table. By then I was slurring from liquor, and it embarrassed me. I didn't hold alcohol well, and I felt like I was at sea, rocking back and forth at half speed. I ran my hand across the back of my neck. I held my breath, and wished I could have five seconds back, thinking how desperate and sad I must sound to this woman who was older, sarcastic and slinky, who sat there with her mouth open, looking almost sinister, her bottom lip shiny and wet.

The lights rose back to full power and in came Dad, scratching his belly underneath his shirt.

He sat down next to us in the bentwood armchair, which creaked under his weight. He had been on the phone with my mother's lawyer in Bangkok. The lawyer had had trouble locating Dad's phone number among her belongings. His English wasn't very good, and Dad couldn't get much detail about what had happened. This is what I gathered.

"Has he been groping you?" Dad asked, off the topic. He looked at me and grunted. "Just like his old man. Has he asked you to the beach yet? Or to the water slides?"

Marina laughed.

"The boy's cranked."

I made a gurgling sound, then gave him the finger, wagged it in front of his face. From me to him, it was something like an endearment.

"His grandfather, my old man, taught him that," Dad said. "The old man liked to curse. They thought he had that disease where you curse."

I could feel his breath against my ear.

"Well, it'll serve you right tomorrow. You little wet fart."

"I think he's asleep," Marina said.

He slapped his hand against my knee, a bit harder than he needed to.

"Boy, do you want me to drive you home now?" he asked. "Or do you want to spend the night here?"

My eyes fluttered open, then closed.

All I could hear was my father's voice, strong and keening and insistent.

"Yeah," he said, "she'd been in Thailand for the last ten years, working as a missionary and singing in a church choir. First I heard of it. There was no note, says the priest. There was no sign of abnormal behavior. Normal. For Helena, that was always depending on how you looked at it. You were probably too young to remember it. A big scandal, in capital letters. It was in all the papers, on television and radio. Yeah. Labor Day, 1980. In town. Things were fine until then. Sure, we argued. Who doesn't argue? The rumor was that she heard the voice of God at a show. Yes, that God. Yes, that's what I gather. I can't say whether that's true. It happened very quickly. I can safely assume that she lost her gourd. She left the tour in the middle of a concert, left everyone in a blur, took a bus or a plane or a dog sled out of town. I held that bag, I did. Nearly bankrupted me. I still had to pay everyone, even if the tour was only half through. The insurance people said there was no clause for holy visions. No kidding. That was the last I heard of her. Didn't write, call. I didn't know she was in Thailand until just now. Last I heard she was in Toronto, living with some Chinese guy. Who knows what she'd been up to? I didn't care, but the boy—it was hard on the boy.

"But no, don't feel as though you should leave. We've been getting along famously, and I think the boy likes you. You can tell. He's a shifty one, a dog, just like his wretched old man. Stay here as long as you want. I insist.

"They asked me what I wanted to do with the body. I told them to bring it over. Bastards. As if they were holding a cake for me. Like that. 'Should we ship it?' They gave me another phone number to call. Then I spoke to the kind priest. His name was Felix. He said he would handle it. Father Felix. Said Helena was a model missionary.

"I'll drive him home, I suppose. He's had a bad day. He deserves to wake up in his own bed.

"The damned kitchen is a mess. Jana had wanted it done for years. She wanted a new house, practically. The woman thought I had gold hidden up my crack, she did. Well, I came into some money just recently and thought I should get it done. Just to prove that I get things done, but when I say they get done. It's going to cost ten thousand dollars.

"You put the salad bowl over there, in one of those cupboards. You shouldn't bother. There. Ha, ha. You're a sweetheart. Ha, ha. You're a gift."

At school, there was an announcement over the PA:

"Boys and girls, before third period begins, I'd like to say a few words. Yesterday, a very serious threat to your safety was made. I'm sure we all know by now what it was. It was a toxic nerve gas threat. And of course many students have been treating this whole thing as a joke—there are many 'humorous' people, it would seem."

In the afternoon, different blocks of students of Frances Brooke Secondary were called for inspection, beginning with those who had the strip of lockers along the hallway dividing the new gymnasium from the rest of the school. Our school was mostly brown kids, some white, and fewer yellow. As far as I knew, I was the only native, even part-native, kid in school. We had specialty-foods days when we sampled samosas and pork buns. We casually approved miscegenation. That wasn't too bad. Actually, when a white kid and an Indian would date, it wasn't terribly scandalous, but it wasn't exactly commonplace. There were skinheads in the school, just like there were hippie and punk kids, but I don't think they were the racist kind of skinheads, just kids with shaved heads who liked the ambiguity. Besides, they were the ones who got picked on. It was the Sikh kids who rarely mixed—there was no great taboo, it just happened. They took most of the AP classes, the calculus and physics courses; they attended the peer-counseling sessions for university entrance. They sent away their transcripts for early admissions. They had hardworking, encouraging parents like Navi's, who wanted him to study law and spoke with half-British accents, like Navi's mother, who was a dentist, or not at all, like Navi's father, a pharmacist with exceptional, delicate manners. I quietly thought some of the Sikh kids obnoxious and loud, thumping basketballs on the concrete courts that were also used for tennis, strolling down the hallways with their beatboxes blaring Indian dance music, bhangra, or hip-hop until an adult stepped out of a classroom and asked them to turn it off. These Sikhs were beefy guys in dark leather sports jackets and track pants. They tooled around in striped and finned Mustangs paid for from summers working at their fathers' construction companies laying concrete for yet another box home. They had full beards at age twelve, swaths of hair between the joints of their fingers and their knuckles. They had bumper stickers declaring "Jat Power" or "Jats Do It Better!" A Jat, according to Navi, was an agrarian caste in India. I asked Navi whether he was a Jat. He didn't know. He didn't hang out with other Sikh kids, just me. We hung out with each other and sometimes Rose. The joke was that Navi and I belonged to the same tribe.

Students were to be at their lockers ready to open them; those who refused would have their locks cut off with bolt cutters. Officer Dale started at one end of the hall, flipping open locker doors with small mirrors and class schedules and pictures of Bollywood stars and singers taped to them, running his hands through suede jackets, rooting through textbooks, water-resistant Discmans, and sour, wrinkly phys ed attire. There was garbage. There were sheaves of loose-leaf paper, empty lunch bags and drink boxes, and darkened fruit rinds, which Officer Dale left on the floor as he made his way down the hall, getting less and less thorough.

"Having a good time, Officer Dale?"

Dale grunted. "I'm having a ball. A fucking ball."

I pointed to my locker, giving it a kick. "It's in here."

Dale sighed. He must have figured, quite correctly, that we had all thrown away our toxic nerve gas fixings. At the open locker next to mine, he nodded absently, his fingers splayed across the side of his sanguine pouch of a face, his chin cupped by the heel of his hand, his elbow resting on his gut, his other arm folded across. He was sighing, looking bored, staring into a gray metal box as if it were speaking to him of desolation, of days like this. He glanced in my direction and shrugged.

"The nerve gas is in here. I've got it here."

I was tempting fate. With my luck, I should have had a big canister of cyanide, or whatever they use, in there, a fat gray keg of death, and people would gawk at me, mouths twisted in shock and scorn. How could such a normal-looking boy, his father this, his mother ran, and then I would be arrested and locked up, so I could think long and hard about what I had done. I winced when Dale opened the door. I bit my lip and scrunched my toes.

A note Rose had written me fluttered out, seesawed in the air.

After the locker search, I met up with Navi, and we left the school grounds. He was slightly shorter than I, but just as bony, with a long, bulbous nose and lashy cow eyes. He was dabbling in fashion these days, having given up T-shirts and high-tops for a more intellectual look—cardigans and tweed, Hush Puppies, and horn-rimmed glasses that he had bought without a prescription at Safeway. He had clumsy, if fine and long, gray hands. In one of them he held a leather case with snap locks and a black plastic handle; inside was his trumpet.

We got lunch at the twenty-four-hour convenience store and gas station across the street. There I deliberated over a selection of iced teas, settling on Lipton, while Navi heated vegetarian Jamaican patties in the microwave by the coffee and espresso makers. By that time, I figured I was on an upswing: my head still hurt, but my stomach had settled. Next to the counter was the local morning tabloid. On the front page was a photo of Helena St. Pierre at an airport, one of those archival shots that imply misfortune by how dated, how seriously outside fashion, the people photographed are. In this picture, she wore a pale-cream trench coat, the belt cinched tight to give her an ass, and wraparound sunglasses. Her hair was parted in the middle and dropped to her waist. Her face seemed narrow. She was alone, one of the few photos of her without my father. Though not really—there he was, in the bottom left corner of the photograph, a hand on her elbow, leading her away.

I waited outside, quaffing iced tea, while Navi paid for his patties. Then we stood under the store's orange sign, next to an orange trash bin, facing empty parking slots and midday traffic.

Anders Wong, our town's only homeless man, was carrying empty pop cans in a Safeway cart.

"Follow me. Let me take you somewhere," he said. "By a ditch is a burlap sack filled with pornography."

"How did you find it?" Navi asked.

"It's my sack." Anders dug out a Mountain Dew can from a trash bin and tossed it in his cart. "The authorities harbor serious hubba-hubba for beaver shots. They'd take it if they found it. It's my prize possession, my oeuvre—but I offer it to you."

"Why?"

"Look at me." Anders brought his face close to us and pointed at himself with his grimy right index finger. His eyes were beady and rimmed with sleep. He had a fine, girlish mouth, and eyebrows that almost came together. Something was stuck to his chin—orange peel. "Look at this face. Can't you see?"

Navi and I looked, stroking our chins until Anders finally gave up on our guessing and blurted out, "I'm in love."

"What's it like?" I asked bashfully.

Anders looked to the ground. He paced around in a circle, his face shriveling in spite.

"My baby's left me for another man. My baby's heart is a lump of coal."

We went to the hardware store at the strip mall down the street. I asked a man in a tie and a blue vest where they kept the spray paint. He gave me a snotty look, chin raised, before leading us down an aisle to the far end of the store. The spray paints were arranged by color, black to yellow, on a rack. I found some gold sparkle and rattled the can in my hand, then started forming imaginary letters in the air, as if I were practicing tai chi, like Rose's parents.

"I don't want to butt in or anything," the man in the vest said, "but you'll be going to court and they'll make you work off the damages. They have records. It'll be damn near impossible to cross the border."

I nodded toward Navi.

"We're painting his sister's bike. Do you have this with more sparkle?"

The guy in the vest shook his head. "Tell it to the judge, boys."

We stood at an intersection, watching elementary school kids crossing. There was a woman across the street at the store. I thought it was Marina, and my heart skipped.

Navi once-overed me with watery eyes. He gulped and gasped. Then his eyes shut as if he were about to sneeze.

"The locker check was heinous," he said. "I'm passing around a petition in protest."

I nodded. He handed me a copy. There were seventy-eight signatures on it already—quite a few of them with the same handwriting. Navi doubted the efficacy of petitions, of conventional methods of change, but he nevertheless felt that the system had to be engaged, that it would crumble under close scrutiny. I believed this, too, maybe with less ardor, but enough to play along.

Navi began crying.

"Your mother killed herself," he said, getting to the heart of the matter.

"That's what they say."

He ran the cuff of his sports jacket along his eyes.

"It's okay." I patted his shoulder. He pulled me into an embrace, and I fell against him, uneasily at first. I envied Navi, how freely his feelings came, and how they sort of fell out of him, perfectly formed.

Then I heard someone call my name. It was Marina at the gas station parking lot.

Anders was talking to her.

"My baby's left me," I heard him say. "She left me for another man. Gone. She made me harder than Cyrillic algebra."

"Maybe I've got the exchange rate wrong or something, but I still don't get it. I mean, why are cigarettes," Marina said, "like, thirty-seven dollars in this country?"

"To pay for health care," I said.

"To kill off the rich," Navi said.

Marina was in a jean jacket with a Skid Row band logo drawn on the back in blue marker. She smiled at me quickly, and the blood rose to my face and my neck.

"I've been sitting around all day," she said, "then I walked into your beautiful town, helped an old man carry groceries to his car, bought cigarettes. Reporters have been ringing all morning. There have been crank calls. Meanwhile Louise is in the study revising her screenplay's first plot point—like she hasn't done that a million times already. Your dad's been taking phone calls, arranging for the funeral. He said the body will be here by Saturday night. That's how long it's going to take to clear customs."

"That long?"

"By then," she said, "the German documentary film crew will have arrived. There's a major TV special in the making."

"I can hardly wait," I said.

But here I was, waiting. Not by choice. We were all sitting around waiting for the world to come to us.

Dinner was the only time someone wasn't playing music in the Samra house, with its creamy plush carpeting and pink wallpaper. Their home was strewn with sheet music, music stands, and banged-up brass and string instruments. Navi was, like me, cursed with a musical family.

The family, including aunts, uncles, and grandparents, ate smorgasbord-style every night—stewed lentils and vegetables in deep aluminum dishes—with paper plates and a patterned vinyl covering over the dining room table. There wasn't a table that could seat the entire family, so we spread out in different rooms around the house, balancing our food on our laps. I sat on a scratchy yellow linen couch in the family room between Navi and his twelve-year-old sister, Priti, while Marvin and Kavie lay in front of the television playing video games. Edmond looked on, anxious to play.

I'd envied Navi's family since my first sleepover here in sixth grade, in spite of the crowding and the bickering that came with such numbers. I watched Edmond start crying and Navi scowl—his little brother always did this when he couldn't get his way. I still envied Navi.

An old woman—Navi's grandmother, I think, visiting from India—sat in a folding chair and talked on a wireless phone. She told Marvin to let Edmond have his turn at the Sony PlayStation. Marvin was an ugly kid with a droopy nose and a bowl cut—it was tragic. He was the only person allowed to play the Steinway, which he had won at a national competition in Ottawa. Priti, who was tall and wore square, plastic-rimmed glasses, asked me about electives for when she entered high school in September. I urged her to register for Miss Adler's drawing class. Priti's twin sister, Jaya, away that night at a jazz choir rehearsal, was weird and obsessed with uniforms. She was begging her parents to send her to Catholic school. I thought Jaya was prettier, but Priti had a nicer smile. Sandeep, whose long, tangly Vandyke had a lentil stuck to it, walked into the room looking for his wah-wah pedal. Marvin told him that it was upstairs in his room, the one he shared with Edmond and Kavie.

Navi was in a hurry to finish dinner. As we were about to leave, Navi's mom asked us what we were up to.

"We're going to school," Navi said from the front door. The cans of spray paint clinked in my bag. "We're rehearsing a play. *Rhinoceros.*"

"Ionesco," she said. She kissed Navi on the forehead, which made me feel a little sad. "Then have a good practice."

We sat on the bleachers in front of the soccer field, waiting for it to get dark. We sat there flipping through the pictures Navi had taken the day before. They were of confused crowds and men in masks, blurry and underlit. Navi owned a Polaroid and a Nikon he had signed out from the photography club and never returned. He was the official yearbook photographer, or so he told everyone, but I seriously doubted his ability to pull one over on the editorial staff. We all had serious doubts. He was a compulsive picture-taker, even if, in his case, ability staggered behind enthusiasm. He had pictures of outstretched hands and frowns and underwear waistbands. There were other photos from the same roll for us to look at. Pictures of people chewing, shots from behind. Photos of me sleeping, where I looked absolutely blissful, like a newborn corpse.

By now it was almost dark. I had to be at Rose's in fifteen minutes.

We weren't very good at topical slogans: on the staff parking lot, we painted "Live Nude Girls" in hot pink, then "Police State Secondary," and on the wall beside the main entrance, we wrote "Shithead." We stood at the edge of the parking lot and inspected our work.

"Well, what do you think?"

Navi nodded. We tried to keep our expectations low.

"What do you think?" he asked.

In response to censorship, I suggested, we should plan a walkout. Navi liked the idea. In response to book bannings and anonymous threats and the state of the world, I proposed we should all just pack up and leave.

In the distance, we heard some muffled crying, then saw Anders emerge from the dumpster, still sobbing about his baby.

That afternoon Rose had left this note in my locker:

> Hi! Western Civ never ceases to bore me. Mr. Plant is having the class form small groups in order for us to make presentations on various systems of government on Thursday. I think he's—as you would say—"on crack" and doesn't want to teach. I'm sorry I yelled at you yesterday. [Here she drew a frowning face.] I was having a bad day. For second period, we're going on a trip to the planetarium. I feel a little old for the planetarium, but still think it will be fun!!! I won't see you today, but I need to

talk to you. It's important!!! Tried calling you last night, but you weren't home. xoxo

Rose lived in a new development, where the houses had three-car garages, with Lexuses and Range Rovers parked outside. There were wide front yards cluttered with shrubbery and pine saplings attached to wooden stakes, but few gardens, sometimes only arrangements of rocks where flowers should have been. She had a separate entrance to her suite. Her parents had it built when her aunt lived with them—until she married a geologist and moved to the Yukon.

When Rose answered her door that night, she was in sweats, her hair in pigtails. The light outside clicked on. A motion detector lit up whenever anything moved in the backyard.

"You're late," she said. "Take off your boots."

I sat on her bed and yanked off my boots. I put my jacket, an English-style rain jacket, at the foot of her narrow bed, and moved aside a geography textbook and placed it on her nightstand atop her radio alarm clock with the lime-green LED display.

Rose stood in front of me, leaning against my knee. I placed my cold hands up her sweatshirt and ran them along her soft belly; I could feel her quiver. She smiled, then backed away and went into her bathroom.

I heard the tap run, then the motion of her toothbrush. It was a wonderful sound, the sound of her spearmint breath. This was what I liked most about her house, about her—not only the cleanliness, but the effort, the energy put into removing the grimy and unsavory.

The bathroom door slid open. Rose came out flossing her teeth.

She sat next to me on the bed, and I put my arm around her waist. She gave off a scrubbed, pink heat.

I fell on top of her.

Rose didn't ask any questions about Helena St. Pierre. She knew me well enough not to, and I appreciated that. I lifted the sweatshirt over her head and let her undo her bra. We lay down on the very narrow bed, my back almost pressed against the wall as we tangled limbs, her short fingernails grazing down my chest.

"I'm getting fat again."

"I haven't noticed."

She had been sick for two months, at home much of that time, alone or with her dad, who took a leave of absence to feed her cream of mushroom soup and watch movies with her as the afternoon sun crossed over their living room skylight. And when she had come back to school, her body, which had been almost boxy, finally matched her mother's quarter-Gypsy face—her dark hair, her soft, doughy cheeks, and eyebrows that arched on her forehead like the legs of a spider.

Rose's head was flat against her neck so that she had a double chin. And there was a film coating her eyes that seemed childish, but immeasurably beguiling, if only because I knew how to make it disappear, to make her feel good.

"How do you like being kissed?" I asked her.

"I don't know. I just like being kissed."

"Like this?"

"That's nice."

"Thank you."

She rubbed her knee against my crotch and put her head against my chest.

"What are you thinking?" she asked.

The light clicked on outside. Sometimes cats or raccoons would run through the yard, and the light would seep through her curtains.

I lied and said I didn't know.

"What do you mean, you don't know?"

"I don't really think hard about what I'm thinking," I said.

"What do you mean by that?" she asked.

"I don't know. I just said it."

"Why don't you ever ask me what I'm thinking?"

"I respect other people's mysteries."

"If I died, would you miss me?"

I nodded.

"Would you be really upset?"

I nodded again.

Somebody knocked at the door, the one connecting the rest of the house to Rose's suite.

"It's my mom," she said. "She probably heard us talking."

"Don't answer."

"She's knocking."

"If you don't answer, she'll think you're asleep."

"It's only nine-thirty. She'll just keep knocking."

"Be quiet."

"Okay."

"Quiet."

I could only picture her cast in smog, half lit, surrounded by a huddle of men, blocked by someone's head. The priest my father spoke to said she worked with young women. In the sixties—almost two lives ago—she'd learned to make dresses from her grandmother and picked up beauty tips and poise from work. She'd sold makeup at a cosmetics counter at the Bay. That was her last job. She'd been trained in women's work. In Thailand she did light secretarial tasks, taught some English, gave sewing classes.

She liked to watch cartoons. During the summer, in the unbroken humidity, they would sit outside under the palm trees, in the field near the church. The girls waved fans and drank from cans of cherry soda. They watched cartoons dubbed into Thai on a television wheeled out from the Sunday school. She and the nuns hung back on hard classroom chairs. The nuns would go to bed first. She would stay outside as long as the cartoons played, often until she fell asleep. Those days when she slept, it was difficult to wake her. Sometimes the girls would have to shake her.

One night, she found herself being tickled. Two of the younger girls were running their hands along her ribs. She twisted, half awake, and fell to the ground, her mouth open. The girls shrieked in laughter. Leni's eyes followed them until they ran back into the dorm, hand in hand.

According to reports, Helena St. Pierre died shortly after an encounter with a television crew.

Once, out of curiosity, she managed to get into a sex club—it was a slow night. She paid the teenage bouncer with the faint mustachio a few extra baht and was let into a room where she saw them in the adjoining room, almost as if in a pageant, in identical gowns. Yellow gowns with numbered badges. When she worked at the Bay in the sixties, she'd been given a uniform with a badge on it, and occasionally she'd modeled swimwear—it had all seemed so innocent back then.

There were two tourists in the room with her—an Asian and a European. The European pulled out a disposable camera, aimed, and snapped. The announcer in the room eagle-clawed his mike, whispered over his shoulder, and the photographer was out on his rear, pushed through the bar, facedown on the street.

It had never been easy for her. It was in her best interests to hear her voice at the dry cleaner's.

A reporter arrived at her door, seeking an interview. This came four days after she'd heard her voice playing outside a bar, two days after the priest approached her with a magazine and a pen. She heard her tune hummed by one of her girls, and stared at her cockeyed.

They—*they*—wanted humiliation memorialized. Their video-tape slathered the air around them, around you, in formaldehyde. They were like ancient pharaohs: killing you as though to place you in their own graves, for you to serve them in the netherworld. Fearing death, they killed you.

WEDNESDAY

Marina put Louise in a headlock. She kissed the side of her head, just above the temple. Louise curled up on the couch and dropped her head in Marina's lap. Her eyes were wet. Louise began laughing, then Marina. They squealed until they were gasping, their eyes merry. Marina carried her long, steep nose with aplomb, her blondness, bangs cut straight across her head, set against her pale-gray eyes. Louise was thin and had a face the shape of a pumpkin seed, her chin pointing out abruptly. Her mouth was too small for her small face.

I had decided to cut class for the day, and went to my father's. I couldn't think straight, I couldn't sleep, and I figured this was the place to be.

"There was an argument last night," Marina said.

Trust Dad to pick a fight, I thought. Trust him to cause trouble.

"We were sitting around," Louise said. "Ian was reading his hate mail. He said I was looking at him funny. I asked him what he meant. 'Oh, nothing. You're just looking at me funny.'"

Louise started to cry.

"I mean, who wouldn't want to be told they were loved?" Marina asked. "Even if they didn't feel the same way."

Louise disentangled herself from Marina. She flipped through a magazine on her lap with one hand, chewed the thumbnail of the other.

"I think he wants to sleep with you," she said.

"Do you think?"

Louise glared at Marina.

"Don't get so excited," she said. A shadow fell across her face. "I only said he might because I wanted to see how you would react."

"How'd I do?"

Louise snorted.

I looked out the window, my stomach growling. It was alarmingly bright outside. The sun had begun hitching its way up the sky, which was a bleached, blurry white, daylight ringing off windshields of cars trickling along the highway, giving the furry evergreen in the yard a stout, overdressed appearance. Dad was outside speaking to a man with spiky hennaed hair. The man wore a pressed white shirt; the top three buttons were undone, exposing pinkish skin.

"That's Richard," Louise said. "He arrived early this morning to produce a segment for German television."

Richard was gesturing royally, his hands above his head, waving them like a television weatherman in front of an imaginary map. Dad looked serious; his gut was flung out, and he scratched his head thoughtfully. He was pointing to the distance, to cow pastures with run-down fencing, past a billboard beside the highway that advertised car rentals.

"The old man likes being on TV," I said.

"Yeah, we figured," Marina said.

Louise ran her palm over her almond-shaped, almost Asian eyes. She was in a cheery red polka-dot blouse; the sleeves were unbuttoned and slipped from her elbows. She rubbed the back of her neck and frowned.

Louise stood up and rolled her neck along her shoulders. She raised her hands, palms out, toward the ceiling and yawned. She bent down and stood on her hands, exposing a flat white belly and pink ankle socks. Her feet in the air, she gave a wobbly smile.

"What are you doing?" Marina asked.

"Giving a damn."

The coffeemaker sat on the counter beside a piece of orange tarp and the old gutted kitchen sink. Dad wanted to know whether I wanted anything. He offered me coffee, which I declined, then took his with cream. Dad's visitors and Richard were going to Pappalardi's, a local diner. Dad said he didn't have time for breakfast, there was business that needed looking after, but that I should go with them before heading off to school.

"Do you think I should be in Thailand?" he asked.

I shrugged. I was taller than he was, thinner. I stared at his bare feet and saw gray hair on his toes.

"Look at me when I talk to you," he said. "I feel like you're trying to sell me a car."

"Sure."

"Do you know how much a fucking flight to Thailand costs?"

"I don't know, Dad." I looked around the demolished kitchen. "Ten thousand dollars?"

"That's very funny."

"Hey, no one's asking you to go."

"I'm just worried about you. I don't want this whole business to be too much bother," he said. "School's important. Look at me. I didn't go to school. You can see what a sorry wreck I am."

My mind drifted during Dad's stab at self-deprecation. There were tools on the kitchen counter left there by Gord. I picked up a tape measure and started yanking it out a foot, then letting it slide back into the metal casing. Dad snapped the measure away from me and put it back on the counter.

"Would you please not play with all this crap. It's bad enough that Gord stopped working on it yesterday."

"Is he sick?"

"Nadine's been hospitalized. I tell the woman the hamburger was fully cooked, but she insists otherwise. 'Well, have it your way,' I say to her."

"Have you heard anything from the lawyers?" I asked.

"Your mother wasn't rich. Don't worry about that. We were surprised she had any money at all. Not a lot, less after taxes and legal costs, but what little she had she'd decided to give to the Church. You'd think the woman would've taken better care of herself. She was living in a sty."

Dad took a sip of his coffee, then chuckled into his favorite mug, the one with the Edward Hopper diner scene reproduced on the side.

"That sounds funny," he said. "Didn't that sound funny?"

"What?"

"When I called Helena your mother."

"What?"

"Forget about it."

"Get to the point."

"You cutting classes, hanging around here. You didn't even know the woman."

"She was my mother."

"Jana's your mother. I mean, I don't know why you're so upset. Or is this your way of getting attention."

He set his mug at the edge of the counter, beside the sink filled with dishes that Louise had yet to attend to, and turned away. I swatted the mug to the ground with an open fist. It broke into three pieces.

"What do you want from me? What do you expect from me?" My voice rose high and nasal like his.

Dad turned back, his face red and startled.

"For Christ's sake, Saulie—if you're going to sulk."

"Dad, help me out here."

"I'll help you. Sure, that's what I'm here for. I'm everyone's fucking wet nurse."

"If she's not my mother, who is she?"

"What is wrong with you?" Dad said. It was as though I blinked just to catch his spit in my eye. "Oh, Christ. Please don't cry."

"I'm not crying."

"Yeah, whatever."

He knitted his brow and his chest heaved. He bent down to the floor and picked up two pieces of the mug, then held them together to see whether they could be attached with glue. The handle piece still lay on the ground. I lifted my foot and kicked it with my toe across the room. It skidded along the linoleum, then stopped near the kitchen table, whose chairs were stacked top.

"What is this?" Dad said. I lunged at him like a grade-school bully, and then fell back at the last moment. I saw my cowardly father wince, an open hand raised in front of his face.

"Who the hell was she?" I asked.

"Who?"

"My mother."

"Not who you think she was." Dad mumbled something under his breath. "We're having a funeral for her. I figured it would be more dignified than leaving her out on the curb."

Richard bought us omelets and hotcakes at Pappalardi's, a family restaurant popular with old people in sun hats and white belts, which featured servers scooting around in mushroom-gravy-brown uniforms, serving French toast or returning with extra cream. I smothered my bacon with maple syrup from a dispenser that got my fingers all sticky, and ate quickly, finishing my order of hotcakes before my orange juice arrived. Richard sat stewing, unable to smoke his hand-rolled cigarettes inside, worried that his cameraman, Andreas, whom he was to meet that afternoon, had missed a connection in Boston.

"So, how long have you been a reporter?" Louise asked.

Richard looked at her, not exactly glaring, his forehead wrinkling in irritation. It took him a moment to collect himself, his face softening again, before he could answer.

"I am not a reporter, even if my background might suggest journalist. There is not exactly a word for it in your language. My position at the network roughly translates as 'cultural critic.'"

"We have cultural critics here, too," Marina said. A waitress was removing our dishes. Richard once-overed her, then looked away.

"My English is poor," he said. "I am more like a cultural *interrogator.*"

"That's what they're called," Louise offered. "Cultural critics."

"They told me I was too good-looking to be taken seriously," Richard said.

"You proved them wrong," Louise said.

"I hosted a prize show in which contestants won money for medical treatments. The contestants had serious ailments— cancer or AIDS, whatever. They were asked to climb the third-highest mountain in the country. Or to pull a car with their teeth.

They—the network—said test audiences found my melancholy preposterous."

"Wrong again."

Richard ran the heel of his hand along the back of his neck, his mouth set sternly. "Yeah, their assumptions proved false. This is true." He said this matter-of-factly, his consonants hard and vowels swift. He was a pretty man, his cheekbones prominent and teeth gapped. He moved his hands effeminately as he filled out his credit card receipt. I listened to Richard talk about Helena St. Pierre—uncovering and handling her life had become his obsession, he said—and I wondered what my own claim on her was. Maybe my father was right—I was acting out for sympathy. But I heard her name spoken and felt a twinge.

"She was born left-handed, but taught by priests to write with her other hand," Richard was saying. "Her childhood pet was an Irish setter named Toby. She had bad teeth, which had to be capped twice. She fell off a bike as a child and had a discolored front tooth, like Indian corn—ha, ha. Her first sexual experience was at age twelve, with a boy at school named Leonard who offered her grape soda. She was an exhibitionist, she called polyester slacks patriarchal. She never had a driver's license. Her favorite color was white. When she was hospitalized, she only ate foods that were white—toast and butter and skim milk. She collected postcards when she first started touring. Later, tours and concerts would be delayed because she would be hiding. In closets, in movie theaters. She arrived in Thailand in 1982. Her grandmother's dying wish—she died in 1991—was that she return to her family. She was an artist; she made people cut her food for her."

The waitress took the bill. We left the restaurant and headed to Richard's car. Marina wanted to know whether I would join them in the city this afternoon. Part of Richard's assignment in Western Canada involved covering Urethra Franklin's tour, which had already included shows in Toronto and Montreal the past weekend, and would include a concert in town Saturday.

"The Franklins are at the CD superstore in the city," Marina said. "They're going to have a press conference and autograph session after a short acoustic set."

"Aren't they an electronic band?" I asked.

"I think they'll be blowing seashells or something."

Richard's rental car was parked at the end of the drag, in the lot of the IGA. Much pride was taken in our renewed downtown core. There was the main drag with its brick and limestone façades, the fire hydrants newly painted red with white trim, the Home Hardware outlet, and the midget elm trees fenced in black wrought iron. Banners hung from the streetlights: "Renewing Our Past!" and "Free Weekend Parking!" and "Visit the Harbour-front Mall!" A fire station had been converted into the new heritage museum, a place where one could learn about the native population that inhabited the area in the first part of the nineteenth century, and about an early Chinese settlement, former railroad laborers and destitute prospectors, whose plywood shacks burned down in the 1890s after a stove exploded. The only building to survive that fire was the brothel, which had become the fire station. Across the street from the museum was Pappalardi's.

The car was in sight when we turned to see Louise in front of a used-book store. She was squatting under the awning, scratching her finger against the window and cooing at a marmalade-colored cat balled up in a wicker basket inside. It stood, arched its back, and raced along the display in front of a hardcover edition of *The St. Pierres' Story* by Leslie Erickson. The dust jacket, faded, with coffee stains splashed across it, featured a picture of my parents. This was what happened when you achieved notoriety: You gained objecthood, you became a coaster. In the photo, my mother, her chin obscured by a microphone, held a tambourine at her hip, while my father, in a turtleneck, shadowy behind the spotlight, sullenly strummed a twelve-string. The same picture could be found on the cover of, and in the photo insert within, the paperback edition I owned, which I kept squirreled away with a pile of photographs of my mother and an old pair of jeans that belonged to her.

"You don't mind," Louise asked, "if I take a look inside?"

Richard wanted to call his cameraman; Marina stayed underneath the green awning to finish a cigarette. Louise pushed the door open and crossed an infrared tripwire, which announced her presence with two electronic bell chimes. The cat jumped out from the front window and disappeared behind the counter.

I followed her in. The store was narrow, like all the other shops on this strip, and smelled of sandalwood. The owner was an Asian man in his forties. He was wearing a Killdozer T-shirt and a shaggy gray beard. His eyes followed Louise as she browsed through paperback romances and spy thrillers in the bargain bin.

I took the copy of the St. Pierres' biography from the display window and looked through it. In perfect honesty, the only book I had read all the way might have been my parents' biography, which I picked up every month or so. I would slog through the boring trivia about their first record contract, and the critical analyses of their first album, *A Home on Blind River*, and their second, *Prairie Winds*, which was recorded on honey slides—hash panfried with honey—and their more electric third album, the megahit *Bushmills Threnody*, from 1973. There was commentary about CRTC legislation, which set quotas for Canadian music on commercial radio stations, and how this altered Canadian folk music the same way Bob Dylan did in America when he plugged in a Fender Telecaster at the 1965 Newport Folk Festival.

I handled the book gingerly.

Say you never knew your mother, and say when she killed herself you felt bad in some ways, but maybe you didn't feel bad enough. Because you were not sure whether you hated her as your father did. And say she was gorgeous.

Say your mother was a model, a conceptual artist, a teenager who had moved to Toronto in 1969. She was already making a name for herself through her public displays of nudity, posing on street corners, in front of a department store, in the name of peace. She was like that—mouth gaping for attention, for what she would eventually throw away.

Your father had also recently arrived, from Winnipeg, via Fort William, where he had been doing Beatles and Kinks covers at a place called the Red Eye. He'd traveled out there in a retired ambulance. His weekends were spent on Yonge Street, in taverns called Le Coq d'Or and the Colonial, gigging with an R&B group called the Resistors because everyone else in the band was a draft dodger. His grandfather had died and left a small legacy, enough to buy a twelve-string Guild. Your father would write his songs in bed, drinking jasmine tea, spitting tea leaves onto the floor of his room, where they gathered next to dustballs and paperbacks. During the week, he would skulk around Yorkville to watch the folkies perform in ill-lit cafés and communes. Near Gerrard was the Bohemian Embassy, where singers served as comic relief between poetry readings, and on Avenue Road was the New Gates of Cleve, where you might find Joni Mitchell, fresh out of art school in the Prairies, or the Tysons singing "Four Strong Winds" or something new that Gordon Lightfoot had just written, or Neil

Young at Club Bluenote with the Mynah Birds (named after a coffeehouse with a nude chef), his band with Rick James here from Buffalo to avoid naval duty.

And one evening your father is onstage at an unlicensed basement venue, singing a number he wrote about his sister who died of polio—another great pain that goes undisclosed—when he catches your mother flicking past the beaded entrance, floating behind a tasseled lamp, talking to some pantywaist who everyone here knows is a painter or writer or something. And your father thinks he can rub out van Gogh with his fretting hand tied behind his back.

His voice cracks. He sings too softly, your father the drunk, the gutter mouth, with a straight face:

> *I want to know what secret takes hold*
> *When she turns away*
> *I want to know what weighs on her soul*
> *When she doesn't say*
>
> *What hurt she must know, a doubling hole*
> *Grows inside her heart*
> *What hurt in her wakes, inside her aches*
> *What is torn apart?*
>
> *Shining brightly, shining lightly*
> *Her eyes warm my eyes*
>
> *For if I had it, the secret to her sadness*
> *I would hide it far away*
> *To the stars above, I would fill her heart with love*
> *now and every day*

Shining brightly, shining lightly
Her eyes warm my eyes
Shimmering lovely, glimmering lovely
Her eyes warm my eyes

Your mother, fresh off a bad relationship, eats it up.

"Are you much of a reader?" Louise asked.

"Not really," I said.

Louise smirked. She reached into her pocket and found an elastic, then pulled her hair back. I watched her rub the back of her neck, her fingers grazing a hickey, and go toward the rear of the store. Her dark ponytail bobbed like a shiny fishing lure. I followed her.

We were facing a narrow shelf of books. At the top, written in red ink on a lined index card, was "Canadian Literature."

"I can't say I read too much, either," Louise said, putting down a copy of *Owls in the Family.*

"But you're a writer."

"Screenwriter. Letter writer."

"Same shit, different piles."

"That's the problem with the world."

"What is?" I asked.

"Too many writers, not enough readers."

Louise bent down, fingering the spines of books.

"That's the problem with your father," she said. "There aren't enough people willing to listen to his story. They would sooner make up their own. That's why your father wants to talk."

"Of course he does."

"If he were so terrible, like everyone says, people wouldn't care about him. Your mother, your stepmother."

"Should I call you Mom?"

"I think Marina has her eye on him."

I absolutely loathed her.

"Forget about it, all right," she said. "Pretend this conversation never happened. At least you're keeping her occupied—for now. That I'm glad about."

"What does that mean?"

"It means," she said, plucking a paperback from the shelf, "that I've found my book, so now we can leave."

At the counter, the guy in the Killdozer shirt rang up Louise's purchase, *hmm*ing approval of her selection.

Marina and Richard were waiting for us outside.

"Can you drive me home, back to Ian's?" Louise asked.

"What did you buy?" Marina asked.

Louise held up the book. The title was familiar: *Baroque-a-Nova.*

"This nerve gas threat someone called in," I said, "was over that."

"Never read it," Marina said.

"I've been meaning to read it," Louise said. "It's Cancon."

"What?"

"Canadian content," Louise said.

She shook her head at Marina, the American, who stuck her tongue out and huffed, "Don't be like that. Just because I can't tell you what the capital of Moose Jaw is. I'm not expected to know everything."

Richard drove only Japanese cars. For that reason I was in the driver's seat of his maroon Ford Tempo when Marina pointed out the sign to me. We had turned at the town's main intersection and were passing the high green fencing that blocked off the highway from the housing developments. I turned back to see.

Seagulls were circling in the sky above. The message was written on a bedsheet in pink lettering: "Helena St. Pierre: 1950–1998." Since my own father thought I was making a big deal of the whole situation, I didn't know why anyone else would give a damn. Maybe there were people here who were moved by her voice. They saw her play live and went home with her voice in their heads. Maybe they owned her albums, clipped out her photos. Maybe they straightened their hair to look like her. Or they paid money to join the official St. Pierres Appreciation Society, located in Thurso, Scotland. Or maybe it was their parents who raised them on Helena St. Pierre, maybe they grew up with her. Imagine that. I looked at that crude sign with more wonder than it probably deserved, as though it were directed at me. An invitation. I didn't know under which terms I could accept it.

Richard pointed to the Silver and Gold Motor Inn, where he was staying. It was obscured by tall spruces, but one could still make out the domed structure, painted lime-green, long faded, that housed its tennis courts, and beside that, a billboard flashing the time and temperature.

"Wednesday is karaoke night," he said.

"Ooh, karaoke night," Marina said.

Richard's spirits had picked up after he learned that his cameraman was on a standby flight and would arrive in time for the press conference. He looked sunny in the passenger-side front seat, wearing his designer sunglasses, holding a bottle of iced cappuccino.

"I look forward to interviewing Saul for my show."

"That's if he's interested," Marina said. She caught my eye in the rearview mirror, and I looked at her as if she was joking. "He seems like the interview-shy type. He keeps his cards against his chest. That's why I like him."

"People show much fascination in the children," he said, sounding defensive. When he brooded, he seemed to be chewing the inside of his mouth. "Of course, all children are humorous when young, because of the regrettable errors they make in grammar and pronunciation. But the children of tragic people, their suffering illuminates. Their tragedy is much like an inheritance."

"Tough titty."

"We must have the child."

We drove past walls of evergreens, the coastal mountains framing the horizon, moving beneath overpasses and beside their grassy knolls, yellow and patchy, until we reached the city limits and the highway ended. Richard rolled down the window and let the warm air whip back his hair as he read aloud the signs we passed. "'Please report vanpool violators,'" he said, chuckling. "'Caution when amber lights are flashing.'" "'Now entering a nuclear-free zone.'" He had a right to be happy, I thought. He was only visiting.

A woman with a large videocamera on her shoulder stood before a mirrored wall at the CD superstore. She fixed her hair and thrust her chest forward before aiming the camera at her reflection. A red light flickered on the machine—it was recording. She began speaking in French, Quebec French, into the foam-headed mike in her hand. The woman was short and curvy, with hair the color of pink candy floss. She was wearing a white spaghetti-strap top, emblazoned with a picture of a teddy bear at the center, and a pair of black clamdiggers.

I recognized her. She was Ramona, a VJ for the French-language music channel. She looked younger in person, almost my age, and a little pastier in complexion. I had pretty much lost the French I'd learned from my grandparents, but I knew she was speaking about Urethra Franklin, something about an award. Every third sentence or so, her rapid Québécois would stop at a clangorous English expression like "Hot Rocks" or "sound check."

"She's pretty, isn't she?" Marina said.

She *was* pretty hot.

Marina nodded as if reading my mind. "You're right."

"What do you mean?" I asked.

"I can tell you like her."

"I don't like her."

"Liar."

There were a dozen other reporters and cameramen huddled before the stage in a casual, prework way. Richard's press credentials allowed us to get past security. We were to stand off to the side of the stage. Richard's head snaked back and forth in search of his cameraman, until his eyes settled on someone. He sighed with relief—more a yelp, really. He pointed to a man wearing a black leather vest, whose hair was combed over. "There he is," Richard said, and excused himself.

We caught the last three songs of the Franklins' set, ending with my mother's recycled voice, which I braced myself to hear. Their version of "Bushmills" was catchy, this was true. I had hated it the first time I heard it, but couldn't get it out of my head afterward. It was a scale-model version of genius, how people could do that—my dad had once had such a gift. Of course, half the Franklins' song came ready-made, sampled. But for everyone else, Helena St. Pierre's voice was background noise. For me, it was the toothache in my heart, the cavity and the filling.

I stood there stunned, as I always did, until roadies—skinny, efficient men in ponytails and black jeans, their heads bowed—

stepped onto the stage, removing amplifiers and turntables. A long table and microphones were being placed on the stage, which took up only a tiny corner of the store, a complex the size of a warehouse, its ceilings fabulously high, television screens ten feet tall above the payment counters and the bag check. Urethra Franklin stood in the background talking to a woman with a note-board and a walkie-talkie. The band consisted of three members. I knew their names from TV: Rob, who was middle-aged and tanned the color of rosewood, played keyboards; Dorit, a round girl wearing Lennon specs, was the drummer; and Hugo, who was of Turkish extraction, his neck long and head shaved so that he resembled a ferret, the rapper with those rhymes about Che Guevara and Michel Foucault. Beside them were two middle-aged native men. One was squat, the other tall, both with thick arms and heavy black hair. The tall one wore tinted glasses and a suit, and kept putting a fist to his mouth and coughing loudly. The squat one next to him wore a white jacket and chef's hat, an easy smile on his face—all incisors.

The store had been two-thirds full when we arrived. Now there were people milling outside, not yet allowed to come in, banging against one another anxiously. The crowd inside began to rush the stage, and ran into security and the reporters already assembled. I was pushed toward the stars onstage. Then I pushed myself toward them, toward their foreign smiles. I tugged Marina along with me.

Most of the group's fans were either teenage girls wearing sparkly eye shadow and tracksuits or older men in leather biker jackets. The younger fans brought along their mothers. They wore their hair stylishly, slicked back or highlighted, and took turns peeping at their watches.

One little girl was staring at me.

"Are you native?" She asked this with a serious look on her face.

I nodded.

"When I grow up, I'm going to be native, too."

A hyperactive man wearing a Molson Canadian T-shirt and sunglasses was standing among the reporters. As he talked, his elbow caught the girl in her eye. She began to cry silently, her mouth yapping open like a little bird ready to be fed. "Shit," the reporter said. "Shit." He pulled out a twenty-dollar bill from his wallet and tried to fold it into her hand.

"Excuse me."

It was Ramona.

"Like, I need to use the washroom, okay? May I ask you to watch my camera?"

I nodded.

"I can trust you, eh? You look clean. You won't run away with my camera?"

She left me no chance to answer before thrusting the camera at me. It was large and unexpectedly heavy, with a leather handle. Then she gave me her microphone, with its spongy head and the French-language music channel's logo on it. Ramona disappeared to the back of the store, running girlishly.

Marina smiled scornfully. "Look at you. Camera Man—he who keeps his eyes trained on the sizzle. Holding the camera for the television personality. I think Frenchy looks a little bloated. She's got an ass the size of a tractor-trailer. But hey, you're the one who's got to live with himself the next day." She made kissing sounds. "Maybe she likes you, Saul. That wouldn't be hard for me to believe. You really do have a knack with the ladies."

"I'm my father's son."

"Ha, ha."

Marina snatched the microphone from my hand and moved in front of the camera, jutting her chest out like Ramona. I aimed the camera at her, watching her through the viewfinder, grainy blue.

"Hello, my name is Jen, Jen Ackroyd from Danbury, Connecticut. I'm honored to have made the quarterfinal stage of the preliminary spokesmodel competition. Fucking mind-blowing. Excuse me, can we start the fucking tape again? Here we go again, nimrods. The presentation I'd like to make is about popular music. Unless you're a bloody mongoloid, you know popular music is good, because people around the world like it, and it brings us together. That's why it's not called *unpopular* music. Hello—popularity? See, that's the point. Hello—community? Hello—liberty? Hello—safety from Quaker militias? The band we're talking to today goes by the handle U Franklin. *U* standing for a part of the body that's, you know, *down there*. Franklin, as in one of our founding fathers. They're responsible for a *rilly* sweet-assed song called 'Bushmills Threnody.' I don't want to ruin anything for you, but it's, like, total *fuck-me* music. They didn't write it, or even sing it. These, like, Canadians wrote it and sang it, but U Franklin have made it better, because they put drum machines to it and they rap over it. Anyway, I wouldn't recommend listening to music made before 1996—a lot of it was recorded by people who have *now passed away*."

At that moment, a man in sunglasses, the same one who had tried to bribe the little girl, stepped onstage. He began speaking into a headset mike in front of the table. He tapped the microphone before him—a thud came from the PA. An automatic camera whined and snapped as he introduced himself—he was the DJ at a local top-forty station. "How is everyone here today? Yeah, well, swell to hear. I see a lot of students here today. What is this, a Professional Day? God bless the public school system."

The DJ introduced the band members individually, to applause and howls. They assembled onstage, then took their seats behind the table. I strained toward them. They looked so lifelike. The flashbulbs really began to light.

I saw Ramona behind us, shoving through the crowd, her platform heels clapping against the floor, utter pissed-ivity covering her pretty, round face. She stood on her toes. We were at the side of the stage, and she could barely see over the heads of other onlookers.

She took the microphone from Marina and clamped the camera onto her shoulder, pressing the red record button on the machine.

Rob the keyboardist stood up and said a few words.

"We gratefully accept this award. It is a tremendous honor."

He returned to the table. Reporters began yelling out questions. Rob the keyboardist would point at one of them, and the crowd would struggle, and generally fail, to hear the question. The band members would pause and consult one another, then the keyboardist would answer into a mike. And we hung on his every word.

"Yes. Yes. This is true."

"No, we are still looking at scripts. If we see one, we will consider it."

"Yes, Hugo was joking."

"The question concerned our influences. Our parents, the music of your Helena St. Pierre, Marcel Duchamp, your McLuhan, Tarkovsky. We met a taxi driver this week who said that his dental work was paid for by faith in God and his winnings at the grey-hound track. He is a purveyor of aesthetic bliss, and my most recent influence."

"Entirely not."

"We have an opportunity to do this. This is good."

"What you say might be true, but if that were the case, then it has been unintentional, more a realization of dreamlike desire."

"Our dreams are like confetti."

"Completely false."

Rob then urged onto the stage the two native men who had accompanied the band.

"I must add," he was saying, "and we have repeated this many times while here, that we feel especially close to the people from this country. We feel a strong connection to your natural settings, to the authenticity of your native people. We sing that 'property is crime.' We learn that from your native people, especially our new friends." He nodded to the two men. "Property, the desire to profit from it, threatens every relationship, even as we speak. It saddens us. I speak for the group, completely. We have thus decided to extend our support to our two friends, Ricky and Ezra Sinclair."

The two men announced plans to block a bridge in North Vancouver that Friday to demonstrate an unfair land treaty. Cameras started taping again as they explained how, to publicize the event, they were planning to bake the world's largest quiche in the parking lot of a nearby mall. "People," Ezra said, "have also been unfair to fat. It is a necessary part of a diet."

"One's body exists in the world," Ricky continued, "yet the world lives through the mind."

Cameras flashed again, and hands were raised, but Ricky and Ezra returned to their places against the back wall.

"One more question," Rob the keyboardist announced.

He scanned the crowd; reporters were waving small tape recorders in their hands. His attention turned to the side of the stage, his gaze falling on Ramona, who was at the very edge of the stage.

"Tell us your feelings about the death of Helena St. Pierre," Ramona said, before pointing her mike in his direction. "Please speak good English."

"We know only her voice," Rob said. "That said, we feel that she was murdered by her scumbag husband."

The two native men nodded in agreement, and then Rob thanked us for coming.

My hand fell to my side.

When we returned from the city, Richard and Marina persuaded Dad and Louise to come to karaoke night with us. I decided not to argue with them, for they were keen on warbling to recorded music with an enthusiasm reserved for onetime affairs. Why not? There was nothing better to do, no other entertainment within a fifteen-minute drive. There was five- and ten-pin bowling, there were water slides, there was this.

Every Wednesday, they came in jackets and leather clip-on ties and sequin cocktail dresses, sip Tom Collinses and house-special double martinis, to watch their friends and co-workers perform on the sunken stage and black-and-white-checkered dance floor, the disco ball hanging sullen and unused above it. We managed to secure one of the last empty booths against the brick wall at the Silver and Gold lounge, with plush magenta seats and our very own personal oil lamp, away from the singles swarming around the bar.

Dad and Louise had arrived early, and Dad was several glasses into Cutty Sark.

"It's because of that damned song," he said, "that I can't order a glass of Irish whiskey without some drunk serenading me."

A thought crossed my mind. "I bet someone sings it tonight."

I didn't know why it seemed so repulsive, but it did, more than the actual record, German remix or otherwise, could. I slumped in my seat, stomach upset, convinced it would happen, waiting for it to happen. Dad had the same look on his face, ashen and sour. I remembered what Urethra Franklin had said about Dad being a murderer, whose actions—the drug use, the domineering behavior, the emotional abuse revealed in the unauthorized biography— somehow inexplicably forced her suicide eighteen years later. I stared at my father, sizing him up, much as I had done that morning. He didn't have that much power.

We watched two men singing "Love Shack."

A woman wearing a feather boa singing "Life Is a Highway."

Three brothers in matching tank tops singing "Wild Eyes" by the Stampeders.

A fat guy singing "Your Cheatin' Heart."

Two hippie girls singing "Shiny Happy People."

Another guy singing "Sweet Caroline."

"You're looking bored," Marina said to me. "You don't want to be here, do you? I dragged you here, didn't I?"

I shook my head.

Dad sat across from Marina, a slippery smile on his face. Marina just stared into her drink, playing with her straw.

"I once fell in love with a man while drinking margaritas," she shouted over the music. "We were in a pretentious Cuban restaurant. He said he wouldn't kick me out of bed for putting ice in my beer." We watched Richard and Andreas singing Springsteen onstage. She smiled, a rare, unguarded smile that made me jealous of her memory. "It only lasted a summer. I liked the way he walked, he walked as though he were in a wading pool, but there were problems, irresolvable problems." She paused, lowering her voice. "I was a slut."

Dad went to the bar.

"Do you mind?" Louise said to Marina, once he was out of earshot. "Or are you intent on giving everyone in the room a hard-on?"

"I'm not doing anything," Marina said. "He's looking at me."

Louise snorted.

"That's what you said about Henri the architect. I can see perfectly well, thank you, and I want you to stop it."

"Okay, okay," Marina said. She excused herself from the table.

Richard and Andreas returned to the table after their rendition of "I'm on Fire."

"Do you like the Boss?" Richard asked us. "He is like bran."

My father came back from the bar, carrying two pints of stout. He placed one in front of me.

"Hey."

I nodded, though I kept my eyes from his. He put a hand on the top of my head, then dropped it.

He mumbled something, but gave up on me and sat down next to Louise, his attentions returning to her. She blushed in the watery, amber light of our oil lamp.

Richard tapped me on the shoulder. He clinked his mug against mine.

"I speak to you on Friday," he said.

He drank four pints of ale quickly, emptying the glasses, his cameraman Andreas, who didn't know a word of English, pounding them back alongside him. Richard wiped his mouth with the cuff of his sleeve.

"Let me speak to you Friday," he said, as though I hadn't heard him the first time, or would be more inclined to agree if he repeated what he'd said.

"I have to be at school," I replied. Trying to be helpful, I added, "We've planned a demo to protest censorship on Friday. You can tape that."

"Then Saturday, yeah. On Friday I must tape the large quiche. It must be Saturday."

"It might not be Saturday."

"This is very disorganized," Richard blurted out bitterly.

He clapped twice to get the attention of a passing waitress. She stopped, cupped a hand against her ear like she couldn't hear, and continued on her way. Richard fumed. When the waitress did return, Richard ordered another pint of Kokanee. "In a clean glass, this time," he said. The waitress put forth her frostiest smile and asked me if I wanted something to eat. I ran my fingers across the foggy, vinyl-covered menu and decided to try the jalapeño poppers.

A man with a baritone singing "Stayin' Alive."

A skinny East Indian man singing "No Time" by the Guess Who.

A woman singing "Two Becomes One."

A man singing "Ohio."

A man singing "It Ain't Me, Babe," the Johnny Cash arrangement.

Louise and my father speaking closely, their hands under the table.

"What do you think, am I insensitive? Do you think I should be in Thailand?" he asked.

Louise wagged her head left and right. "You need to be here."

"Do you know how much a fucking ticket costs? Especially if you don't make reservations two weeks in advance?"

"A mint, I'd bet."

My father nodded smugly, and it seemed then, for the very first time, his hatred for Helena St. Pierre really surfaced. Of course, this wasn't true. He had filled a twenty-year-long separation with his empty slights, but it was the first time I looked at him and figured that he probably had wished her dead. I felt my face turn red.

Richard and his cameraman slid out of the booth and let me out. I approached the dance floor next to the stage, where Marina was flipping through the song catalogues, sipping a margarita. As I approached the dance floor, flakes of light fell on her like confetti.

"You look angry," she said.

I was angry because it had happened. Someone began singing "Bushmills Threnody," the original arrangement. She was a heavyset woman who occasionally lagged half a beat behind. The stage lights switched from orange to purple. She stood by a prompter, which scrolled out the lyrics on a television screen, the words highlighted in pink as they were sung:

> *I try to forget about you*
> *But you write, you telephone too*
> *Oh, my dear,*
> *Your hands so soft*
> *How can I sleep you off*
> *Like a hangover from the night before?*

> *I used to see you first thing in the morning*
> *And the last thing I heard was you saying good night*
> *So how could you be so cruel?*

When you said I was playing you
That I've been making you out to be the fool

The crowd held still, all of them aware of recent events, a few even recognizing my father. They kept their eyes fixed on their drinks—including Jana, who had just arrived with Officer Dale and taken a table on the other side of the room, away from Dad and his young girlfriend—as if extraneous movement would heighten the embarrassment.

I could almost hear Dad start in on his stories about the song. Dad only ever talked about that song. How he wrote it in his room at the Roger Miller King of the Road Motel in Nashville, on tour in support of a second album, nursing a nasty case of stomach flu. How he had to insist on having the song on the record, because Leni, my mother, fresh off another mental breakdown, which saw her hospitalized for three weeks in April 1973, thought the song too sappy and self-pitying. "Sappy? Melodramatic?" my father screamed. "That would suit you fine. That song is you." He laughed at her. And then he promised, if the tune made the top ten, knowing full well it would be a B-side, he'd start a family like Leni wanted, because that was what she wanted; that was sup-posed to make her happy and content.

My heart sinking.

My mouth dry. It didn't matter that this woman mumbled off-key and sweated under the stage lights. You couldn't go around pretending you were my mother. I wouldn't stand for it. The woman onstage could've been a remarkable singer, and she could've been the most beautiful woman in the world, with a voice like a canary or a skylark or a nightingale, a voice to which poetry aspired, and it wouldn't have mattered. Because Dad was right— Helena St. Pierre was that song. Everyone thought so. Or at least

I did. You could sing the same words, but it was a poor imperson-ation, just like you could put on my mother's clothes, her cowboy boots, her dashiki, her fringe jacket, the white gown she wore on her last tour, the one with the ruffled taffeta collar, but still get it completely, perfectly wrong. It made sense that Urethra Franklin had sampled my mother's voice.

I left the bar and stood stone-faced outside in the parking lot. I sat in Richard's rental car, ready to leave, staying there for half an hour, until everybody was willing to go. Dad was right. Every word of it was her, every crack of her voice, every ragged, weary sigh was my mother, who the world knew was dead.

THURSDAY

The lunch bell sounded, and my classmates, in their summer peasant dresses and sandals, their cutoffs and Converse All-Stars, their Tevas, muscle shirts, and pylon-orange track shorts, went outside. They were baring brown and mocha and pasty off-pink and bronze and tawny skin. They began trickling out from classrooms, taking their plastic containers with celery sticks spread with superchunk peanut butter, and sprout-and-feta sandwiches in unlabeled brown bags past the paper and glass recycling bins. They went by the posters advertising the yoga club meetings and the native-style mural painted on a cafeteria wall featuring the raven, the school mascot, so they could eat outside under the languorous sun, which rationed its visits to this area.

I was trying to live half an inch under my own skin.

Rose stood by my locker, reading a book.

"You're not allowed to read that," I said, moving past her, turning my back toward her like I was afraid she would steal my locker combination.

"Says who?" Rose said. She put the book into her bag. "My parents say we should be allowed to read what we want."

"Good for them."

I opened my locker, then realized I didn't need anything from it. I already had on my rain jacket, which I always wore until it became too warm to bear. And I certainly was in no mood to study. I shut the locker door and stepped away from Rose. She took hold of my jacket sleeve.

"I tried calling you last night," she said.

"Was it important?"

"I just wanted to talk."

"About what?"

"Nothing."

"Well, I'm here. Why don't you tell me now?"

"What if I said I'm pregnant?"

Her chin was bunched and her gorgeous eyebrows knit together. I had upset her, her eyes were set a certain way. She wanted to yell at me, but wouldn't because she was that close to crying. She was wearing a baggy sweater and sweatpants—clothes that she was starting to fill out again.

I hated her.

"Jesus," I said, yanking my arm away from her, almost reflexively. I wanted to take it back, but we stood there, Rose's hand held up in reproach.

"You're not really, are you?" I asked. "Tell me you're not."

She shook her head.

"I'm not," she said.

"Thank you."

She gulped and started breathing heavily as if to calm herself down. "I wanted to talk."

I walked past her, my gray backpack catching against her chin. She winced and put her hand to her face. I felt helplessly mean, cruel by default.

"People do that," she said.

I turned around and her eyes were wet.

"What?"

"They talk."

I squinted at her angrily, out of exasperation. "That's all they ever do."

The band room, where Navi, Hedda—the anarchist from Olympia, Washington—and I held our lunch-hour walkout information session, was designed like a theater, with terraced levels that ascended from the conductor's podium at the front to the percussion section, with its large bass drum and xylophone prominent, at the back. I took a seat near the front, where the brass section sat. On the floor was a photocopied flute part for "Mack the Knife." A brown shoeprint was stamped across it. I watched Navi on the podium, his slender shoulders hunched, halting but then gaining momentum as he continued speaking, periodically raising his head from his index cards and smiling brightly at his audience. Thirteen people showed up to hear Navi give his reasons for the planned action: he listed the civil liberties that had been infringed on when our lockers were searched and when students were questioned by policemen, not to mention the book censorship that lay behind the alleged toxic nerve gas threat. He underscored the necessity of direct action. He had done his research and briefly quoted Veblen and Bakunin from lined yellow index cards.

"In short," he said, before beginning the discussion period, "the discourse of power precludes privacy and free thought."

Navi's oratorical skills were accentuated, perhaps slightly unhinged, by his appearance. In a bow tie and a green velveteen blazer, he fostered the image of a man who had other things on his mind. His hair was slicked back, and even from where I sat, I could smell the Listerine on his breath. This was the same person who one Halloween night as a ten-year-old roamed our misty, amber-lit streets as Orville Redenbacher, popcorn magnate.

Navi: student, photo artist, poet, musician, disruptive element. He liked people and planning events, and had confidence in his own ability to cajole and organize. Before his revolutionary aspirations, there had been team sports like softball and soccer. There had been Hot Dog Day, which he single-handedly revived, and record-setting UNICEF drives. There had been go-carts and video arcades, summer fairs where I'd lose him in flashing lights and stale candy floss and carnival music.

Hedda spoke about making T-shirts that would read, "Frances Brooke Secondary, Inmate #_____" or "Kill Your Inner Cop." Navi wanted publicity. He had called both local dailies and a television station in the city, but had yet to hear back. Hedda had also enlisted something called Rent-a-Mob, a group of university students who, given twenty-four hours' notice, would come to any protest ready "to meet all your activist needs." There were plans for a barbecue and a live band, Throws Like a Girl, a straight-edge group at whose squat Hedda was staying. The walk-out was to be a community event that extended past the school, where Navi's posters had been taken down an hour after they were posted. I was to re-poster Friday morning and had crowd-control duties during the event. He assigned the responsibilities for new posters to three ninth-graders, two girls with nose piercings and hemp wristbands, and another in a bomber jacket and army boots, who encircled him like a pack of lapdogs and spoke in anxious, breathy tones.

"Completely off the topic," I said to Navi, skimming my finger along his velveteen jacket, "but may I add that you're looking especially spiffy today?"

"Sometimes you have to look your best," Navi said, "to unlock the champion inside."

"You really look as if you deserve a prize."

For the rest of lunch hour after the information session broke up, Hedda, Navi, and I sat outside on the gray wooden bleachers with other students. Bhangra was playing out of a car CD player in the parking lot behind us, Indian singers accompanied by dance beats. The track and soccer field lay in front of us underneath the deep blue sky, which was dotted with seagulls and lined with narrow wisps of cloud, jagged as shark's teeth. Past the field, on a corner at the edge of the school grounds, was a baseball diamond. A waist-high chain-link fence separated the school from generous backyards—from their aboveground swimming pools and swing sets, an occasional trampoline, too.

Hedda was a heavy woman in goth makeup, with shoulder-length black hair that framed her face. She was sweet and weirdly giggly, and she sort of treated Navi and me like kid brothers. She brought us lunches, chocolate soy milk in juice boxes and egg salad sandwiches on crustless whole-wheat.

She had driven across the border in a rusty green El Torino station wagon to help us out. On the way here, she had picked up a hitchhiker south of Seattle who told her dozens of bad jokes, all of which she related to us. "So a writer is in a car with his mistress," she said. "The mistress is driving. The writer looks out the window, then says to her, 'You're passionate.' 'Oh, how sweet,' the mistress says. 'No, no,' the writer says. 'You're passhing the likkur shtoor.'"

We sat on the bleachers drinking chocolate milk, listening to Hedda's jokes and reading her zine, *Pig Abattoir*. Navi was featured in the latest issue. He had published a poem, "Absence":

i do not have a cat
it has no shape no mass no color
nor a soul for that matter
it did not act differently after it was neutered
because i did not have it neutered

i do not have a cat

its meow is indefinable
it hits eleven and one-half microtones
in frequencies
heard by both narwhals and unicorns
(its forefathers often possessed this meow)

the cat does not scratch out my eyes
nor does it evoke fond childhood memories

O cat, you do not comfort me
(as better cats do)
but I will label you neither good nor bad

Accompanying the poem was a photo-study entitled "Studies of Absence," comprising six blurry photos of a marmalade-colored cat in a wicker basket. Cats were not allowed in Navi's house on account of his mother's allergies, a situation that brought Navi not a little grief.

"*Pig Abattoir,*" Navi said, "has subscribers in New Zealand and the Caribbean."

"It's not a big deal, really," Hedda said. "Not if you get into the right circles. Find conventions, acquire favorable reviews. Meet other people who write letters and trade zines by mail. I'm trying to put it on-line, but I think it might alienate some of my friends."

"*Pig Abattoir* has three Amish subscribers."

"Avenues of communication are being advanced, while our words—the substance of thought, the currency of imagination—are stripped away from us, by illiteracy and ad copy, because thoughtfulness, discretion, diversity stand in opposition to the profit margin. People opt for corporation-modulated, systematized living situations because they see no choice."

"They give you a choice of Pepsi or Coke, as if those are your only two options. In place of choice, we get a soft-drink binary."

Hedda smirked and smiled—one of those killer, secret smiles that women deploy strategically, intricate and coy, like a playing card facedown. She offered me a mandarin orange. I declined. She ate it herself, ripping into the orange's skin with her long black fingernails. "I hated high school," she said. "I tried killing myself twice in my senior year. I mixed Southern Comfort with my stepmother's Valium. The zine saved my fucking life."

"*Pig Abattoir*'s about being your own spokesperson," Navi said. "Being your own hero. We try our best to reach out to high school kids who'd otherwise find religion—one of those cranky religions."

Our graffiti from two days back was already gone, whitewashed over by custodians the following morning. No one had been caught yet.

"What's the damned book about?" Hedda asked.

"It's hard to explain," Navi said. I'm pretty sure he hadn't read it. "You're going to have to read it yourself."

Hedda smirked again as if daring to call his bluff. "I've got T-shirts to get done for tomorrow."

As I was leaving school, I passed Anders Wong, one hand on his bottle-laden shopping cart, at the pay phone outside the store. Anders kept clicking the receiver.

"I need twenty-five cents," he said. Anders was a stocky man. He was wearing a turquoise turtleneck sweater and an unflattering pair of spandex bicycle shorts. He had an odd odor, though not exactly a bad one—like the way someone's clothes might smell after a night around a campfire.

"I've got to call," Anders said. "I see her in my dreams; I see her in the arms of another man. My baby doesn't pick up the phone. My baby's not home. She's with him. She left in the middle of the night. She ran away to be with him, the man who wrote that book. I don't hear her voice anymore."

He told me he'd been trying to use this phone since nine-thirty.

In the bottom of my trouser pockets I found a quarter. Anders took the coin and fingered it in his palm before dropping it into the machine.

"I'm a dangerous man, Saul."

"Why?"

"I have my reasons."

There was the sound of a voice on the other end of the line, distant and gray, then Anders making what I figured to be his usual toxic nerve gas threats.

It was the warmest day of the year so far, and even as I walked into a breeze, I could feel my T-shirt sticking to the small of my back. I went along Trunk Road until it intersected with the highway, then took the overpass, which presented the lazy midday traffic as it passed through our town, and the flat, shingled roofs of our houses.

It was written in pink block letters, not on a bedsheet, but on a piece of white tarp fastened with cord: "Helena St. Pierre: 1950–1998." This incontrovertible fact, so harsh and wrong, a matter of public record. The cord was tightly double-knotted, and difficult to untangle. My hands were raw when the first knot began to loosen. I wondered whether anyone would have expected it to come to this—whether my mother had given much thought to me, whether she had ever imagined me standing here right now.

She was the remarkable half of a minor celebrity couple, her voice a prairie wind in February, when winter settles on the land like an uninvited houseguest on his hundredth night, a native woman who was so shy she would sit alone in a dark room or in a bus for hours before a show, who would beg her husband to cancel tours. On-air tributes to my mother included old film footage from their tour, the big one that followed the success of "Bush-mills" in 1974, black-and-white stills from their folksinging days. Her reclusive nature was underscored—her disappearance after a 1980 Labor Day show, which nearly caused a riot because of a withheld encore.

Her death was like the sound of a stone falling into a well long after it has disappeared.

I folded the tarp into a square and stuffed it into my knapsack.

The cars stopped at the intersection, and I gripped the rail and leaned forward, collecting spit in my mouth for the most contemptible blue BMW 325 in recent memory.

I felt something on the back of my neck, dropping on me. I put my hand to my neck. It felt wet and grimy. I looked above to the seagulls circling, going about their business. Business as usual.

Dad and Andreas were in the front room preparing for their interview. Andreas was moving furniture, Dad clipping a microphone to his shirt. "You're going to like this," Dad said to me, staring into his chest. "I'm going to pour my bleeding heart out." He almost cackled. I shrugged. Dad had the front room decked out like some shrine. Above his chair, on the mantel of his gray-brick fireplace, was his Juno Award for "Bushmills" and a picture of Dad sitting at a table in a Greek restaurant with Warren Zevon, the woman who played Bailey Quarters on *WKRP in Cincinnati,* and the guy who owned the restaurant. Above these souvenirs was the Gretsch White Falcon, the big hollow-body with a shiny silver whang bar I'd admired as a five-year-old, the same guitar he used on tours and recordings when he wasn't playing his twelve-string. It was mounted on the wall like a large polished fish.

"You should charge admission," I said.

There was a hole in the front window, which faced the residential street and the shrubbed cul-de-sac. Dad had taped a sheet of cardboard over it with gaffer tape until it could be repaired.

"Dad, you been getting death threats?"

"Why sure," he answered cheerfully. "Isn't everyone?"

Richard bounced into the room, wearing his makeup. His reddish face was powdered, and there was something girly about his eyelashes—they were curled. He had so much powder on his face that he looked like a bloody mime.

"Yeah, totally radical," he said. "We discuss the music, we establish the time and place through sprightly montage. We play memorable clips, television appearances."

"We'll clear the air with this. People think I'm the Ike Turner of Canada," Dad said. "No one knows what happened. No one fucking cares. It's a native-rights issue, it's a feminist issue. They want to throw bricks and UPS hate mail to my front door. You should see it. I have a stack of angry correspondence piled on my desk. This morning, I had to sign for a box of dog shit. There are people out to get me. I'm not afraid of them—well, there's this one guy."

"Who?"

"There's this large man somewhere who wants to rape me. Either that or shoot me."

"No joke?"

"I don't joke about large men."

Richard's hennaed hair was gelled up into spikes. He was still wearing a white bib over his black silk shirt. On his neck was a small gob of shaving cream. He pointed to me.

"I speak to you tomorrow, is good?"

I shook my head. Richard sighed loudly, then looked to my father.

"Think it over," Dad said. "Say your piece. No one's going to force you to say anything."

Andreas was adjusting a light next to the fireplace. He spoke German to Richard, who nodded.

"It is agreed," Richard said. "We must have the child."

The hallway floorboards creaked as I approached my old bedroom. Across the hall was my dad's room. The walls were thin. When I was still living with my father I could hear every word of his fights with Jana. By that time they had stopped caring who was listening. I would stare at the stucco ceiling and the plain white ceiling lamp, round and antiseptic like a urinal cake, the crickets chirping outside my window, its scratchy blue curtains drawn.

The door to my father's room was open. Louise lay on his unmade bed, napping. A pillow had fallen onto the brown carpet, and the white dress she had worn at the barbecue was folded over a chair next to the desk—on which Dad's hate mail was heaped like a paper pagoda. Louise was curled up, in a black T-shirt and khaki shorts, her head resting on the underside of her forearm. Her laptop sat open beside her, its screen blue and flickering.

Jana and I had moved out of the house quickly. Jana left all her books, titles like *The Moving Finger* by Agatha Christie, *Play As You Learn Bridge*, *The Essential Gardener*, on the living room shelves beside the leather-bound encyclopedias, her clothes in the closet, and, in a basket hanging in the shower, hair and bath products, conditioner and extra-fancy gels and fruity soaps, which Dad had yet to throw away. We had left the undersized desk from my room and taken only the bed. My posters were still hanging—a map of the world, a hockey poster, a guide to sign language that a man on the street had sold me. I looked at my room: it seemed as if I had been waiting for it to be occupied by strangers.

A foldout cot was set up in it. Marina sat there cross-legged, reading Louise's copy of *Baroque-a-Nova*. She put the book down, spine-up on the cot, beside a blue airline pillow on the open sleeping bag.

Louise was still mad at her, Marina was saying, still jealous that she would steal my father.

"She's driving with her emergency brake on, if you know what I mean."

"How is it?" I pointed at the book. I sat down beside her and crossed my own legs.

"It's like a Romeo and Juliet story spanning two hundred years of Canadian history. Flashbacks, flash-forwards. I get the feeling I'm missing out a lot. Like the use of weather in this novel." She picked up the book and flipped through it. "'It was twenty below at Portage and Main'—page six. 'The snow fluttered down onto rooftops like moths who had tired in their ascent toward the sun'—page twenty-seven. What's the fascination with weather in your country?"

"The typical fascination."

Marina laughed. She thought this was funny. And I sat amazed at how unpredictably her laughter came, how thin-lipped and deadpan she was until it did. She folded one leg further into the other, the wonky metal cot creaking as she got into the lotus position. She was always crossing her legs and moving. I liked that about her.

She stood, in a pair of Converse high-tops, five feet, six inches. Or just under 168 centimeters. My best guess was that she weighed between 100 (45.5 kilograms) and 130 pounds (59 kilograms). She looked resplendent in a tank top. She smelled like orange Jell-O or peach bubble gum. She liked to use the word "wicked." She was blonde and American, from the northeastern area—her *r*'s occasionally flattened, so that "wicked harsh" sounded like "wicked hawsh"—and she complained mildly about how homogenized milk tasted funny in Canada. She was grim and sardonic and fucked up—albeit in a mortally attractive way. She appreciated attempts to communicate and behave with authenticity. She listened to the horrible music of my parents, folkies turned rock balladeers, a habit that had seemed very odd but was starting to make sense, or was maybe something I had just accepted because my parents' music, perhaps crass, was sad and stirring. She might be teasing me. Or perhaps she sort of liked me. She'd mentioned last night how she quit smoking pot when she was twelve, because she didn't approve of "that culture." But she adored margaritas and daiquiris, summer drinks she consumed with a speed and gusto that belied their essential girliness.

All signs would indicate that she was here on earth to make a difficult situation worse—to be the object of a lustful crush, to distract me from the untimely death of my mother, the anger I felt toward my father, and the ambivalence for my sort-of girlfriend.

How do you seduce an older woman? I wanted to know this badly. This was valuable information.

The last image of my mother is of her hand, then a door closing. During Richard's interview, he plays this for my father on a fourteen-inch monitor Andreas has set up on a coffee table between Richard's and Dad's armchairs. Dad is in a buttoned-up denim shirt and cowboy boots, his silver hair tied in a ponytail. Is he wearing makeup, too? I'm not sure. Richard does his German spiel, his introductory remarks, addressing the camera directly. The rest of the interview is in English, to be dubbed or subtitled in the future. On the monitor is footage shot recently, of Dad at home, Dad driving around, Dad playing "Four Strong Winds" on his Guild. It is the kind of footage you expect to see, but it seems false and staged when the person shown puttering around is your father.

"Where have you been?" Richard asks. And Dad shakes his head.

Where has he been? He has been hanging around. He has raised a kid, remarried, and divorced again. He has set roots. There were comeback albums—two of them—and a third attempt given up halfway through the first recording day, when he figured his reedy voice would never inspire the hearts of radio listeners. Of course there was the song for starving Africans—he sang his one line after Geddy Lee from Rush—there was his one acting job, the guest appearance on *The Littlest Hobo*, typecast as a down-on-his-luck musician befriended by the Hobo, Canada's Lassie, a guileless, slack-jawed German shepherd. There were small club dates with other female singers. There was a jazz vocalist who owned a dozen feather boas, a big-haired Texan who flew in because she had dreamed lucidly about playing with him on an all-lavender stage, a twenty-year-old in leg warmers who hopped on the *Flashdance* wagon a week too late. He was *reinventing his sound.* He was *devoting time to a couple of projects.* But his success was contingent on *her* voice, the voice of a woman whom he had run into one night after a gig in May 1969, and whom he had seen a month later across the street, buying cantaloupe at the first organic grocer in the neighborhood. He chased her down. "Knowledge through pleasure," she said on their first date, wondering if there was a bumper sticker she could find with this written on it. "People don't get it." Of course she didn't have a car, but she could stick it on anybody's bumper. Property is a crime. "Do you know the human body can last forty days without food?" she asked at a Moroccan restaurant. My dad's eyes narrowed merrily. This woman, who had broken up with her boyfriend, was already dating Ned the painter and Hayden who liked ceramics and some guy who etched. But I'm the guitarist, he must have thought, because, in his quiet, unassuming manner, he sort of overwhelmed the competition. I'm the dick artist.

He says, "Richard, Richard, where have I been?" He runs his hand over his hair. There is a hiss in his voice, the bile rising. "Don't even start, Richard."

Richard has a remote control that he uses to run the video clips. There is early performance footage. Dad in a serape and flares. Helena St. Pierre in an orange dashiki.

"I was never comfortable as a folkie. It wasn't me. Show business was performance. It wasn't supposed to be *art*, it wasn't intended to be *truth* or personal revelation, because, from what I knew, those things were unpleasant. It was something you saw or heard, something you went to, that made you happy and entertained you, so you could get through another day at the salt mine without having a go at your foreman with a pickax, so you could go home and not slap your wife and kids. You performed to entertain, not to confess, not to sing about your childhood. You performed because you wanted to be part of something beautiful. I got into music because I wanted to wear a tuxedo like Peter Lawford, my hero. I made my father jealous, because he always wanted to be the performer. He would drink and sing in the morning and cut hair while hungover. I was cruel to my old man. You can rebel against your parents, but it's always on their terms. They say to you, 'This is how you can destroy me,' they hand you a knife and then point to their weak spot, and then you either do it or you don't."

Concerning the performance footage:

"This came about a year after Leni and I met—we knew friends who were supposed to play, but their drummer was stricken with appendicitis two nights earlier. It was for a city television station that wanted local content. I don't remember this taping very well. Only that a cameraman fainted. Of course, this was her doing. She used to make them all faint. Not just girls and swishy little men. But big burly bikers even, who would come to our shows so they could swoon like women at the feet of, you know, Peter Lawford. Later on, she learned how to sing without incurring casualties. She held back."

He holds up a finger, then reaches in his pocket. "Just a sec," he says. Richard lights his cigarette.

"I knew people. There were people to be known. You meet this guy who chants William Burroughs aloud in pig Latin, you stay at this person's girlfriend's loft and studio space, she makes hats out of felt on the side, she knows another guy who plays tabla, so you form a band. This certainly doesn't happen anymore. People don't know one another. I feel sorry, really sorry, for young kids today. We had fun, more than our parents did, more than our kids ever will. My parents certainly didn't enjoy their lives. They were very sad people, especially after my older sister died. Claudette died of polio. It turned my mother, especially, into an atheist. She cursed God in the morning under her breath, scrambling eggs. They complained that we had it so easy. But we did, we were always fucking around. Cigarettes were cheap, cars were cheap, excessive European vacations were cheap. This was a few years before everybody started choking on their vomit—that cruel winter of asphyxiation, 1971. And the music was more interesting, maybe because we were stupider then—we were pompous—but at least we dreamed in grand and obscene terms. Even Toronto, if you can imagine, was like that, so much as Toronto could be like that. It was as though the town had been built on dirty thoughts. Everywhere. Not just the coffeehouses. They were starting up universities left and right, Marshall Plan dollars from the States or something, and they were letting boneheads teach, true weirdos, but these guys were interesting. You might not have learned a whit about Chaucer, but you were given the chance to see a hung-over English prof up close, railing about macrobiotic nutrition and tantric sex. Not that I ever took a university course, but that's what I hear. I don't know, am I rambling?"

"We have a one-hour show," Richard says.

"You could tell how good a time it was, because we dressed like fools. We were deep-sea diving so far up our own assholes that we neglected to observe our glaring dumbness."

"Tell me about her."

"She was crazy."

"Is that all?"

"Come on."

He is sucking his cigarette.

"Of course, everyone knows about this. But sure, allow me to refresh the public consciousness. Leni was already notorious at the time. She'd been posing nude for a class, and one of the students—some guy she knew at the co-op gallery—asked whether he could paint her on a street corner. Downtown Toronto. It would be an event: nudity for peace, art for peace. It was as though peace was something you bought at the deli with your cole slaw. She got into a lot of papers, black bars across her tits—you know, use your imagination. She was arrested for that, fined, then she went out and did it again. This time she was spread out on a couch. I went to that one, everyone did. A naked woman lounging on a divan and no cover charge. She was the most beautiful woman I had ever seen, I grant her that. You met Indian people, yeah right. Everybody those days had an Indian grandmother. Newborn children were being named after entire tribes. Cherokee, Dakota, Cree. But you could tell that she was the real deal. She was a tiny rail-thin creature, but when she looked in my direction—those eyes—I was swallowed alive, the way a snake swallows a goat, the way fat people slurp up fettuccine in white sauce. There she was, in front of the Bay display window, in front of the mannequins. Leni, the performance artist with a sign around her neck that read 'Invisible Mink Coat: One Thousand Dollars.' This was considered revolutionary. Now they hire malnourished teenagers to do it on billboards. Back then, people threw dollar bills at her. They hooted. I might have hooted—who knows? I think her boyfriend threw a punch at me.

"I met Helena Sinclair, I met Leni at a show months later. A friend invited her to see me play. I shook when she approached me; I shuddered in anticipation: she looked better with clothes on.

By then, the nudity had lost its novelty. There was a woman in Ottawa who had set up a naked kissing booth for peace. Nudity was old. She needed something new. She figured all the art she was doing was short-lived. The new art was all about saying, 'Look at this, look how this is art. And if you don't think it's art, that it's gorgeous, then you should be looking differently, you patriarchal fool, you establishment lackey who'll never be loved or appreciated, may your cock drop off your body from neglect.' But the thing was, people get tired of being told where and how to look. It was like church. Who wants to be in church?

"I asked her how she enjoyed the show. She made a face. I wasn't much of a singer, she told me. She was never good at hiding how she felt. She was shy, shy in an aloof, snooty way perhaps, only because she was afraid to let it be known, though she did eventually, that she sang. That's the difference between talent and genius, folks. Apparently, I wrote well enough. My songs were good, if my singing wasn't. She wanted to know whether I would write her a song. When I saw her next, about a week later, I had written the entire first album. It went well. We played. Who knew she had that voice? Who knew she was that good? My prayers were answered. I took her to dinner afterwards because the girl looked like she needed a meal.

"We played our first show soon after. It went well and they asked us back. At our next show, someone came backstage and asked me whether we wanted to make a record. Allan something-or-other, who wore penny loafers with his flares and worked at the record company as the hip talent guy." He snaps his fingers and smiles. "It happened that fast.

"*Blind River* was recorded quickly, almost live in the studio, just minor overdubs, in a dump on Yonge Street, in a room lined with purple egg cartons, with an engineer named Lefty. It was more a demo than a record. The name of the group was the St. Pierres, even if we weren't married yet—not for another four months. She said it had a ring to it. Hint, hint, pun, pun. This was about the time that government agency, the CRTC, instituted quotas of Canadian music, so our stations would promote homegrown talent. To qualify, your songs had to be written by Canadians, the music played by Canadians, recorded in Canada, and produced by a Canadian. You needed two of those four criteria. Or something like that, I forget. Radio stations loved us, simply because we weren't terrible. I won't speak ill of anyone, no names, but the Cancon rules let a lot of shit slide by. Spectacular mediocrity. We were just a good group at the right time, and the legislation helped us out. Period. Well, maybe, we added some harmonium, we sweetened the songs with strings. Because that sells. Sold.

"So we did well, and she seemed happy enough. She liked playing in front of her friends. For our first show, she mailed rainbow-shaped invitations to her TM class. And though she wouldn't have said it, she was as ambitious as anyone. She wanted the love of the world, but she didn't know what to do with it once she had it. She wanted to return it, I think; she wanted to give it back. She complained when we started making money. She wanted to give it away. Give it away. We argued about that. And then there were hospitals—two times. I don't know what they did, but it was a waste of money no matter which way you slice it. The doctors said there wasn't anything wrong with her. They sat with her in a room and asked her to talk, to talk herself to sleep, because they thought she was suffering from insomnia. You don't just quit, you don't walk away. There lay our differences. I couldn't stop working. I wrote every day. I woke up at six with my Guild and—"

"About your wife," Richard says.

"Of course, of course. That's what you want to know."

The camera is square on his face. He scratches his nose.

"I don't know what to say about her death. It's sad, I suppose, but I was surprised, really, that she survived as long as she did. She heard voices. There was something wrong with her."

"Tell me more."

"If I saw her now, I would say, 'Hello, how are you? Didn't we have a good time?' Then, 'See you. Good-bye.' Why she ran out at the Labor Day show with half a tour to play, another twelve dates, I still don't know, won't ever know, don't want to know. We were professionals. So what if she was under stress—that I knew. She saw another doctor about it. He put her on a prescription. Maybe I'm past caring. I wouldn't have any questions. Why bother? Maybe she'd ask me how I've been. She ran out on our son, left him for me to raise. If we met, I would hope she'd ask me about him."

Richard chooses this precise moment to play the last image of Helena St. Pierre. The camera shows a crummy apartment court-yard, where clothes hang drying on lines stretching from one side of the building to the other. It proceeds unsteadily, past barefoot brown children, following Richard as he passes a row of orange doors and barred windows. Richard stops and knocks. A door cracks open, then a hand crowds the screen. She cries.

The voice of Helena St. Pierre asks, "What are you wait-ing for?"

And then the tape stops. There is no more. Richard switches off the monitor.

This is witchcraft, I think, death crawling toward me on hands and knees, frame by frame.

Jana wanted me home for dinner. Maybe she thought it strange that I was spending so much time around Dad, given the situation.

More than a year had passed since we'd moved out, abruptly and bitterly. I remembered hearing the phone ring late that night, my father's rumbling. Then Dad and Jana began to argue. He landed one backhanded slap on Jana that left a bruise along her cheekbone. I woke up that night and opened my bedroom door to find Dad standing in the hallway in a white T-shirt and pajama bottoms, his eyes set on Jana. I remembered disgust whelming in my heart, looking away from his face to the floor and the graying hair on his toes, his red flip-flops. I had lost all faith in him.

We moved out the next day. Jana said she wasn't afraid of him, only that things were getting so bad they had stopped talking, that it wasn't worth it anymore. We stayed with Gord and Nadine before Jana found a townhouse in a complex that sat placidly beside a nursing home and a children's playground. Dad paid half the rent. Jana had recently finished a degree in history after a ten-year break from school. She had to work, so she put in three or four days a week as a temp. She answered phones and took dictation in large offices full of people who took pains not to learn her name. She would be gone once the regular secretary recovered from the flu or got back from Reno. "It seems like my lot in life— to fill in," Jana said then, lying on the living room couch with a comforter up to her neck. When I dropped out of school, we spent a lot of time together, just the two of us on the couch watching daytime TV and feeling glum. She taught me to foxtrot to scratchy Django Reinhardt LPs, and we would dance in the living room, stopping mid-song to move the glass coffee table.

Then one afternoon she told me to get up. It was a big day for both of us, she said. I got showered and dressed. Jana was waiting to go, looking better than she had since the separation. She led me to her car and drove me to school, where, in spite of my weak-willed protests, I re-enrolled in classes. She took me downtown to a salon beside the fish-and-chip house and had her hair high-lighted. She forced me to get a manicure.

She had a date that night. With Officer Dale, whom she'd met at the dry cleaner's. When I saw the smile on her face, I realized how much I depended on her, and that I could say anything to her. After the salon, we bought fish and chips wrapped in cones of newspaper, and ate in the car. There I asked her, for the first time, about my mother, whom everybody knew but me. I was very conscious of my beautified fingernails.

Jana told me that my mother had one day announced she was leaving Ian so she could be alone.

She said she was meeting an old lover, this fellow who had jilted her in Toronto ten years before.

"I told her," Jana said, "that that was no good reason to walk away from anything."

My mother didn't have a better answer.

From Jana's cramped kitchen with the red-tiled floor came the smell of roasted potatoes and curried chicken. She was at the counter, next to the breadmaker, wearing a pair of thick ceramic bracelets, which clicked together as she tossed a salad. On the radio was the maritime fiddle music that made her homesick. I wrapped my arms around her from behind and kissed her soft cheek. It felt powdery and cool. She smiled faintly and asked me to set the table. It was cluttered with newspapers and mail, and two bowls caked with dried-out muesli.

"I have news."

"I hate suspense," I said.

She leaned back against the counter, tight-lipped, her eyes twinkling.

"Dale asked me to marry him."

"So what did you say?"

"Maybe, I told him. Probably. He wants to start a family, he says. Your dad never wanted kids with me."

"Oh. Congratulations."

"Dale likes you, Saulie."

"When are you getting married?"

"Not for a while."

"Good."

She started clearing the table, stacking the newspapers for the recycling bin.

"This place is a mess," Jana said.

"We need a maid," I said, something I instantly regretted. I'd opened myself up to reproach. I began arranging the mail in a separate pile on a chair, then scraping off the gunk from the cereal bowls into the wastebasket and rinsing those selfsame bowls in the sink. I was doing my helpful-stepson impersonation because I was expecting Jana to lay into me, to say I was an incontrovertible slob and that she wasn't my housekeeper—this performance notwithstanding. But instead she sighed, a tired look seeping from inside out to her face.

"We need a bigger kitchen," I said.

"Maybe."

"Does Dale have a big kitchen?"

Jana sighed again. "Not really."

The timer sounded and she pulled the potatoes out of the oven. She poked at them with a fork and wrinkled her nose.

"And your father's finally rebuilding *his* kitchen."

"He had a change of heart."

Jana set the salad on the table. I brought the potatoes from the counter, the hot Corningware scalding my bare hands, and sat down.

"How long has he known this woman?"

"About a week, I guess."

"Hm."

"They wrote him a letter."

"They?"

"She has a friend with her."

"What kind of women would shack up with a middle-aged man after writing a letter to him?"

"The same kind who would run away and join his band when she was seventeen."

Jana clucked in a dismissive way.

"I was never *in* your parents' band. Besides, that doesn't make what she did right. But I suppose you've made your point. Your father is not without his charms."

"There's a large man who wants to rape him."

We sat and ate, quietly at first. Jana told me that Rose had called.

"She's a sweet girl, don't you think?"

I nodded.

Jana frowned. But I knew she'd be displeased if she found out how badly I was treating Rose, so I said nothing. She pouted, something she was not above doing when she didn't get her way. I changed the subject, telling her about the interview and our glimpse of Helena St. Pierre. "It seemed funny that Richard found her, when even Dad didn't have a clue in twenty years."

"Well, you know, they've got satellites," Jana suggested. "Cold War spy technology."

"Oh, come on," I said. "Please."

"I'm not saying they used Cold War spy technology to find her, just that they could, they have the capability."

"Sure."

"Well, maybe they hired a detective. That sounds credible, doesn't it? A detective."

"A gumshoe. A private dick."

"*Saul.*"

"That's what they're called, *Jana.*"

"Fine."

We sat quietly. As another fiddle song faded out on the radio, I added, "Watching Dad interviewed reminded me what a public dick he is."

"*Saul.*"

After dinner, I helped clean up. I covered the leftover potatoes in plastic, put the leftover curried chicken in a container, and then took a dish towel to dry the things Jana had scrubbed. She asked about school, hoping to find a topic for peaceful dishwashing conversation. I mentioned the nerve gas scare, how Navi and I responded with the walkout. Jana giggled. She liked Navi. She thought him polite and sweet, his enthusiasm endearing. He was the type of person who had half-hour conversations with your stepmother about gardening and orthopedic footwear. Navi was a big suck.

"What I like about him," she said, "is how he can turn everything into an event—in a good way, though."

"Some crank phoned in the threat over a book."

"What book?"

"*Baroque-a-Nova*, by Nathan Shaw."

Jana turned off the faucet and set the last plate down. Her eyes narrowed.

"It's been a long time since I heard his name."

The tarp, when unfolded and spread out, more than covered my bed. It extended over the twin-size mattress and hung off the edges.

My fingers traced the words "Helena St. Pierre" and the dates after them. I sat at the edge of my bed, imagining her hands on the rail and then one foot over, a pale calf exposed as she straddled the rail, her stomach puckering, the other foot going over. The air smelling smoggy and foreign to her, as it did before she'd gotten used to it—like car exhaust, incense, or skewered meat.

The light in the room was off. I lay down on the bed, wrapping the tarp around me. I closed my eyes and imagined the same woman screaming at Richard to go away—I tried to think of her at that moment jumping.

In her periphery, the balconies of her immediate neighbors and those next to them, their woks sizzling and their appliances whirring and blaring, loudly eating electricity from 220-volt outlets. In front of her, the ever-smoggy sky covering the midday urban sprawl like a tent made of tightly sewn strips of gauze.

CHAPTER FIVE

FRIDAY

That morning I reread Leslie Erickson's *The St. Pierres' Story*. I kept it under my mattress, secretively, as though it were pornography or contraband. I placed it now on my nightstand next to Nathan Shaw's book.

According to my parents' unauthorized biography, Helena Sinclair was born in central British Columbia on a Shuswap reserve near Williams Lake, and was raised by her maternal grandmother in an unpainted government-built house. Her father had shot himself a week before she was born. A year later, her mother married a white man in Prince Rupert and was, as these stories go, never to be seen again.

Your mother at your age, younger, her skin spotty, eyes squinty but gleaming, her face baby-fat pudgy. Helena is slender, with soft hands and a shy smile. She runs her tongue along her bottom lip. She wears pigtails, lipstick, and a knotted scarf around her neck—in the style of the Italian starlet from a film magazine she lifts off a nun at school. The other girls are afraid of her. They can't ignore her: she runs around in the yard wildly, oblivious to everyone. She climbs trees at night to be alone. It's like she's sort of possessed, bad luck. And the boys, their waists narrow, their intentions transparent, all greasy-headed, *blech*, they don't even rate a mention. They want her, and she lets herself be had occasionally, just for kicks, although she prefers the company of older men. She makes eyes at her high school history teacher, the only lay teacher at the school, the only male. It's fun, it enhances self-esteem, it helps her perfect her walk. Glide, sway, flick your hair. Cover your mouth when you laugh. She meets him on a bank off a hunting trail, carrying an army blanket in her folded cashmere arms, her hair dark and straight and slick.

You think of your mother in positions of weakness.

The history teacher takes her to Vancouver. And she works in the diner of the downtown Hudson's Bay Company department store. This woman is too beautiful. And she's an Indian. Sexy, demure, though maybe a little off-kilter. She doesn't talk and she doesn't spend time with the other girls in the store. She hums to herself.

A manager notices her while she's serving him a chicken pot pie. She smiles meekly because the crust's burnt. Soon thereafter, he makes the one bold decision of his career and awards her a scholarship and places her on the store's "fashion council." She takes the scholarship, of course, because what good is physical beauty if she doesn't use it while it lasts, while men still find her alluring and plausibly innocent.

They give her a green blazer with a "Bay Fashion Council" badge stitched on the breast pocket. Local models arrive Friday afternoon to discuss hygiene, poise, and posture. She's the only native among them. The manager has taken a chance on her, like she's some test-tube experiment for the new cultural mosaic of the coming years. Her craphole apartment is deemed "unseemly," so the store billets her in the home of an appliance salesman ten months away from retirement. They cap her teeth and teach her to model swimwear. They offer to pay her tuition for a degree in commerce, so that she can be the next generation of cosmetics counter manager.

Welcome to 1967.

Your mother works at the perfume counter Mondays to Thursdays from eight a.m. to five p.m., and Saturdays from ten to four, offering samples of blush and mascara beside the cash register. This would be enough to bore anyone to thoroughly gushy tears, but then there's the matter of the high school teacher, who wasn't the grand idea she was hoping him to be, either. He's older than she thought, his body unappealing, and he farts wickedly.

One day at work, it's too much. She's ready to write her grandmother to wire her bus fare home. In the store that day, the Oriental with the taped-together horn-rims and the toque with the earflaps, the creep who's been hanging around her area the past month, is trying to steal a five-ounce bottle of Chanel. She trains her eyes on him as she's been taught to do, until he puts the bottle back on the counter and vanishes behind the Barbour rain jackets in Menswear.

Two hours later, he returns. He hides behind a mannequin and spins the tie rack to the tinkly music. She catches his reflection against a mirrored pillar. He approaches—oh God, what a dope in his bearskin vest, in his flares—how fast can security get here—in his hair that sticks out at the bottom like Mary Tyler Moore's on *The Dick Van Dyke Show*. He drops something on the counter and leaves.

It is a slim collection of poems, Jacques Prévert's *Paroles*, the City Lights edition. She opens the book. As an inscription, someone has written, "You're so cool!"

What does she do? Your mother narrowly averts being caught stealing, leaving work a little early that day, quitting. Her manager, a smile on her as stiff and frosted as her beehive, asks her where she's going. She smiles back at her and walks away. Your mother, eighteen years old, will move to Toronto, where this funny-looking man seeks to write his novel.

Glide, sway, flick your hair.

She sees him on the street outside the Bay. She fingers the bottle of Chanel in the pocket of her purple faux-fur jacket. The store is about to close, so a guard has to unlock the heavy metal door for her and hold it open.

He isn't your father, just the love of your mother's life.

According to Jana, my mother didn't say too much about Nathan Shaw. He wrote books, she told her. They went east together. He was the one who had saved her from department store drudgery.

Jana said she met Helena St. Pierre in July 1980. Jana was seventeen years of age and not yet a high school graduate. The St. Pierres had begun a four-month tour that would see them play forty-two concert halls throughout the continent. It was an ambitious jaunt organized by Ian, who wanted their latest record to crack platinum. His wife had given birth six months before, and already they were back on the road, the child left with his parents. Jana was handed a backstage pass during the Halifax concert and managed to take off with the band the next day, flashing half a smile and promising the road manager good karma if she could catch a lift. She wanted to leave the Maritimes, perhaps for Phoenix, where she had a cousin, or San Francisco or Vancouver. Anyplace west. People there were more relaxed; all the great things were happening out west. She had a feeling she was born ten years too late, but hoped she hadn't entirely missed the good vibes. She met Gord, the pedal-steel player, on her second night. He was sweet and laughed a lot, so in keeping with times past, she decided to be his girlfriend the same way someone might choose toothpaste.

She was lucky. Gord was a sweet man. He kept her away from the road manager and his porno thoughts. He warned her never to touch any equipment, and to stay out of the way. That was fine with her. After the first few nights, she decided not to attend the after-show parties, filled with coke and hash and guest-list flotsam—what she could only assume to be the typical assortment of weirdos, industry people, and sucks. At the heart of all the action was Ian St. Pierre, a man with heavy eyebrows and rounded shoulders, who managed to be simultaneously menacing and sickly, his face puffy and red from scotch, in a powder-purple tuxedo shirt. He would glare at her, those eyes in their own way as striking as his wife's. Like Clint Eastwood's movie-star stare-down, but more sinister, less heroic, shorter. And even if he dressed and acted like a variety-show parody of the gadfly, she felt him looking at her from the pit of her stomach, from behind her knees. She slunk around the buses during sound checks, talking to the local security people and ballroom cocktail waitresses, smoking Gord's Rothmans in the alleys behind the concert halls, hoping to avoid him.

Jana watched Helena St. Pierre sing twenty-nine times during the tour, every single performance ending with a rendition of "Bushmills Threnody." Ian was obliged to play it, though its success was embittering. For even if he was right and he wrote twenty other tunes as good as "Bushmills," he failed to convince radio stations and record buyers of that. By the second week of the tour, he made the touring band rush through the song at one and a half times the tempo of the recorded version, just to get it over with. Somebody joked that the song would soon be renamed "Bushmills Polka."

The band would return for the encore, the stage dark except for a single spotlight on Leni, who stood there teetering, her hands flapping.

Jana thought she was gorgeous, striking and aloof onstage, and was sure she could live her entire life twenty times over without seeing anyone more beautiful, more lonely, enchanting, and sad than Helena St. Pierre. She seemed oblivious to the crowd, yet she would turn away as if she had heard something, someone calling her.

The night before, Jana had told me, reluctantly at first, of how Helena had confided in her during that last tour. They'd watch *Bugs Bunny* and *The Flintstones* on the luxury bus, and my mother would cover her mouth with her long fingers, the nails chewed off from backstage anxieties, and laugh—the only time, my step-mother claimed, that she did. She laughed once for five whole minutes, until her face was purple and Jana was about ready to holler for help, before she said, "Jana, have they hurt you much?"

"Who?"

"Men."

Men who love your mother.

Jana watched them. Ian and Helena. At a state fair, behind a trailer, holding hands, the scent of horse manure from a nearby petting zoo wafting in the humid air. A portable generator buzzing, some megaphone announcement rumbling. It is three hours before the show that night. Just a couple of trailers down, some of the guys in the band are playing pick-up floor hockey on roller skates, with a few sticks, an egg-shaped ball of gaffer's tape for a puck, and orange pylons for goalposts. Ian kisses Helena's forehead, puts one hand inside her shirt, and presses it against her belly.

Ian is not a tall man but he rests his chin on her head.

Or at an airport:

Leni, in her dark glasses, on Valium, heels dragging against the floor. Ian leading her by the elbow to the baggage claim. Maybe she's having a sulk. Maybe it's because she doesn't eat much. Jana's never seen her finish a meal. Leni nibbles.

She jerks her arm away from Ian like a willful rag doll. Ian continues walking maybe ten feet, then turns, waits for her to catch up. Leni seems to look past him, a wobbly smile on her face. She sways, then drops to the floor and begins shaking. Ian crouches beside her, holding her shoulders down to the ground. A seizure. She hasn't had one of these in three years, Ian says, not since her last visit to the hospital. He sounds more irritated than alarmed, treating it like a temper tantrum.

In concert:

He's terrified that this woman can do this to him, that he dies with every dip and swoon of her voice. He is watching Leni, his eyes rounded, his jaw to his knees. His love for her is territorial, like a prospector guarding his stake, his plot, four invisible lines marking the extent of his longing.

On the road:

Ian likes the fact that Leni has a friend, that she and Jana are up watching television together and talking late into the night. Leni has no friends. She's scary, or so everyone has you thinking.

He knocks on Jana's door one night in Baltimore and thanks her for "keeping Helena calm."

"It's my pleasure," Jana manages back.

Leni's knitting needles click as cartoons flicker on the set in the hotel, the two of them sitting, feet up, on a bed in Gord's room. Leni catches Jana from the corner of her eye and smiles.

She talks as though there were someone sleeping in the room, as though she's afraid to wake the person.

Ian and Gord are downstairs in a nightclub or out on a producer's boat. Somewhere with music, a great selection of liquor, a vegetable platter—where there's women and coke. According to Leni, Ian's more of a drinker—when he drinks, that's all he really wants to do—but he plays along. Leni partied with them on the first few tours as her way of relieving stress, but all the rum and Cokes gave her stomachaches. And liquor is fattening, anyway. If she drinks, it's vodka or gin—something clear. She decided the parties were the worst part of touring. That's what she learned from the psychiatrists.

"Am I ruining your night?" Leni asks Jana. "Wouldn't you rather be out with everyone? With Gord?"

Jana shakes her head. "I'm tired."

"Ian was looking for you."

"Why?"

"He wanted to know where you went, silly."

"Oh," Jana says. The bed faces a dresser mirror, which is next to the television. She sees herself blush.

"Do you like being here, on the road?"

"I guess."

"You can go home anytime you want. You know that, don't you?"

"I know. I talked to my parents last week."

"What did you tell them?" Leni asks.

"My parents, you see, I don't know," Jana says. Leni smiles, almost motherly. As waifish as she may look, as badly put together as she can be, Leni's still thirteen years older than Jana. "They're really nice, but they think I'm too young to be away. They think I don't know what I want."

"What do you want?" Leni asks, putting down her knitting. She's making her little boy a red scarf.

"I don't know," Jana says, then starts giggling. She sounds even younger, like a kid talking with candy in her mouth. I must stop laughing like this, she thinks to herself. But Leni doesn't ask these kinds of questions, Jana thinks, not usually. "I sort of want to be away for a while. I like being around the band. I like being around you and Ian."

"Do you want to sing?"

Jana looks Leni square in the eyes, afraid this is some joke, that she's about to burst into laughter.

"No," she says.

"Is it because you don't think you can sing?"

"I have an ugly voice," Jana says. In fact, she used to sing in a choir. She has a fine voice. "You're the one who can sing. You sing beautifully." It takes courage for her to say this to Leni's face, because she has wanted to say it since their first conversation, but didn't lest Leni find it embarrassing or think her another groupie or band hag. And the more she has gotten to know Leni, the wiser she thinks that decision is, but now she goes temporarily imprudent and blurts out her admiration. Leni smiles abashedly, as though an embarrassing secret has been let out. "I cry when I hear you sing. My heart breaks when you sing."

"We'll give you a tambourine," Leni says.

"I don't think I can play tambourine."

"What do you want, then, sweetie?"

The cartoons end. Leni clicks off the TV.

I told her what I wanted, Jana thinks, that I wanted to be here. Maybe she wants me to say something else.

The room is quiet.

"Maybe I don't want anything," Jana says. "I just like being here."

"You might grow tired of it."

"I guess."

"Sometimes I get tired of it," Leni says. "I think maybe I'd be happier if I were by myself."

"With Ian?"

"Don't you ever want to be alone?"

"No." Jana says this without thinking. "I'd rather be with you."

Leni laughs.

"You're a lot like Ian. Ian can't stand being alone, either."

Jana sees her reflection, burning again. She moves over to the edge of the bed and sits away from Leni.

"What is it?"

"I don't think he likes me," Jana says. "He doesn't say much."

"Of course he likes you. He likes you a lot."

"Did he tell you that?" Jana asks, feeling a flutter in her chest. She feels treacherous, considering who she's talking to.

"I'm his wife," Leni says, as if to remind her. "He doesn't need to tell me everything."

"I get the impression, you know, that he doesn't." Then Jana adds, "I mean, I like him."

"You do, don't you?"

"I guess."

"You love him."

Jana starts to apologize: "I'm sorry. I didn't mean—I love you, too. I wouldn't do anything."

She throws her arms around Leni. It's like hugging a hat rack.

"I know you wouldn't."

"I'm sorry."

"I'd like to be alone for a while," Leni says.

"Oh," Jana says, and makes to leave the room.

"I want to get away."

Jana asks where. She stands by the door, not sure whether she should leave.

"I haven't decided yet. I think Ian will be lonely without me. I think he'll be unhappy."

"I'll miss you, too."

"No, you won't. You'll be with him."

Leni resumes knitting. Needles clicking.

As noon approached, it seemed unlikely any crowd would assemble on the soccer field. A lack of excitement was discernible as the young men and women in my English 12 class hit the Off buttons of their cellphones, clicked shut their three-ring binders, kept hip-hop beats with their fingertips on slanted, tortoiseshell-finished desks and with their sandals and sneakers on the burgundy floor, and snapped shut tubes of fluorescent mango-orange lipstick to the sound of the third-period bell, a recorded bleep, solid and unremarkable, playing over the PA.

Outside on the soccer field was one middle-aged man.

I saw Navi's head pop into the classroom as we watched the last hour of *The Handmaid's Tale*.

"The whole third floor had to be postered," he said as we moved through the hallway.

"I forgot," I said. "I'm sorry."

"Oh, well. Fuck, whatever."

We were both glum about the turnout. I watched two, four, ten, fifteen students leaving their classrooms, moving with us to the soccer field. The floor squeaked as we walked.

Navi had a walkie-talkie, not some toy but a professional deal, a rental. I heard Hedda's voice coming from it, staticky and distorted.

"Proceed with Rent-a-Mob," Navi said into it. "Over."

The intention was street theater, a counterspectacle. Beneath the overcast sky, on the bleachers before the soccer field, sat Hedda, wearing a tiara made of aluminum foil, a huge costume-issue ruby necklace, and a strapless ball gown, maroon and crushed velvet, with a sash across it reading "Miss Police State 1998." She held at her side a bullhorn, which she handed over to Navi, who proceeded to direct the thirty-five members of Rent-a-Mob in the middle of the field. Navi, in his bow tie and tuxedo shirt, looked underdressed. There were two or three men in dog collars, two women with neon-blue hair, a man wearing a rubber Pierre Trudeau mask, a woman with a "Take It Sleazy" T-shirt. They held signs carrying abusive slogans, some with no apparent political content, like "Eat My Ass." Someone carried from a piece of cord a five-foot-tall inflatable pig, dressed in a blue policeman's uniform and holding a club. Navi and a couple of Rent-a-Mobbers huddled around a box of fireworks, to be used as a sort of display once the entire crowd was assembled and Navi had given his speech. These days, to assert your presence in the world, you needed really big signs.

"A lot of the guys want to take over the principal's office," Hedda said, nodding toward those in dog collars. "They want to pull the fire alarm so there'll be police in riot gear here, and we can all get maced and get four column inches and headshots in two leading campus newspapers." She checked her watch and shook her head. Navi lit a bottle rocket, shooting it from a Coke can. We watched it go off, screech into a brief flight, then make an abrupt nosedive. "*Boys.*"

I laughed.

"You're looking really nice," I told Hedda.

"Oh, this. I wear this around the squat," she said. "The problem is the other syndicalists don't know how to dress."

"You look really pretty."

"Believe it or not, some guys don't dig fat chicks. I think it's a sign of immaturity."

I was ashamed of myself.

She had a backpack slung across one shoulder.

"Are you hungry?" she said. "I have an apple in here."

"No, thanks."

I didn't see Rose, and I wondered what could be keeping her from this event. Me, probably. The skies were getting darker, the clouds heavier.

More people were assembling on the field. There were now maybe seventy-five students, some perhaps out of curiosity, others wanting to make their stand in the face of authority. I still didn't expect a big crowd.

I heard a boombox playing Urethra Franklin. Somebody among Rent-a-Mob grumbled that the group had sold out. Another person, the one carrying the inflatable pig, suggested that Urethra Franklin used ideology as a pose and that they had no integrity to begin with. Take, for instance, Helena St. Pierre, whose image had been appropriated and commercialized. A third person, the one with the boombox, suggested that it was necessary for the movement to have a common identity—in this case, a theme song. He argued that the balkanized musical tastes of the student population represented a divide-and-conquer tactic promoted by the government, which licensed radio stations. And that choice was, in this case, limiting mass unrest. Another person called the third person an RCMP mole. A fifth person suggested the boombox was stolen and was in fact his. A struggle ensued, during which the fifth person smashed the boombox.

"This is no way for anarchists to behave," said Navi, wincing, well aware of the apparent irony.

Hedda told me I looked like my mother.

"People say I take after my old man."

"My parents used to play the St. Pierres in the trailer park. I would prance around in the gravel yard outside in a home-made tutu with 'Bushmills Threnody,' like, blasting away from the kitchen, my dog Sprinkles—the black Lab we had to give away because we could never housebreak him—prancing around with me."

"I'm not a great fan of their music," I said. "But people seem to enjoy it."

She shrugged.

"You like what you like. There's not enough pleasure to be fussy."

"Good point."

"I'm all about good points, Saul. When I'm alone in my car, I turn on the oldies station. I was driving up here, and this one station wouldn't stop playing that song because of, *you know*. It was the first time I really listened to your mother's voice as an adult, one who's been in love a few times. I almost drove off the road. I had to turn into the next rest area."

The Indo-Canadian Veterans Legion arrived, about a dozen or so rickety old men who eased out of a blue van parked beside the bleachers, using walkers and canes, wearing crumpled suits and wispy white beards. Navi greeted them, shaking each of their hands. Six months before, when a Sikh member had not been allowed in a Legion hall, Navi and I organized a petition at our school, and now they were here to support us. The twelve men lined up on the field, all of them taking hold of a giant banner: "Indo-Canadian Veterans Support Human Rights!"

Navi came over to us on the bleachers.

"I don't see any reporters," he said.

"Whom did you call?" Hedda asked.

"Everyone. They're all at the demo in North Vancouver, taping the quiche."

"Maybe they'll show in a couple of minutes."

"I'm dying out here," Navi said. "Rent-a-Mob is starting to lose interest."

"Is that a reporter?" Hedda pointed to the middle-aged man I'd seen from the classroom.

"Well, he's not holding a camera."

"He can still be a reporter."

"Rent-a-Mob won't be happy about this."

"Rent-a-Mob's a pack of starfuckers."

"I don't think he looks like a reporter."

"Why?"

"He doesn't look very curious."

During the three weeks before they left, he read Wallace Stevens aloud to her on a full-size mattress in his attic room in Kitsilano, until the mattress was sold and they had to sleep on the floor. He had a mass of black hair greasy like one of those reservation boys, she thought.

After they met outside the Bay, he invited her to a party at his co-op, a stocky Victorian near Jericho Beach. The house had a religious theme: the basement floor, where the bicycles and water heater were found, was painted red, the middle floors green and blue, and the attic room, which one could reach only by step-ladder, white. It was a joke among the co-op members, a visual contradiction of the house's faulty heating system, which saw the infernal basement icicle-cold much of the year, and a personal statement by Nathan, the housepainter, whose heavenly room was easily the hottest, with its low slanted ceilings and swampy climate.

That night, in Nathan's room, among his friends, where illicit substances were used, someone picked up a guitar and asked if anyone sang.

Nathan turned to Leni. "You must sing, right?"

Later that night, when she first kissed him, she shivered.

Leni Sinclair follows him to Toronto. They take a train across the country, for two days nipping from a tin-silver flask of Jim Beam to take their minds off the Prairies, the stretches of wheat golden in the afternoon sunlight, and as wide and deep as the sky above, which is at least five shades of blue, and immobile and massive like a block of marble.

Nathan tells her that both of his grandfathers and three great-uncles helped build the railroad.

They refill the whiskey from a twenty-six-ounce bottle in the overhead storage, from Sunday to Tuesday, until they reach Ontario. They sigh together in relief, Leni's head against his arm.

Nathan's working on a new look. He has cut his hair and started wearing a clean dress shirt underneath a blue mack jacket. He looks like a Chinese version of those young American men, their backs stiff against their seats, their eyes fixed determinedly on the border guard as they are asked their citizenship and how long they are staying. He's always kept his fingernails clean. He's taking her to meet his uncle, who runs a greasy spoon near the university, specializing in Chinese and Canadian cuisine. "What's Canadian cuisine?" she asks. He looks at her bitterly.

This is the man your mother loves. Her first love. She puzzles over him. She plays a game. In her mind, she subtracts parts of him: the way he smells; his hands along her back; the sound and quiver of his laugh when her face is clamped to his chest. She tries to locate him among the gestures and words. She subtracts, takes back, and dissects until he is faceless, nothing. She does this over and over again, building him back up.

He is sharp and at times short-tempered. The week before, he doused her with a glass of lukewarm water during an argument.

Miss you, she thinks, is a tautology.

She is a total sucker.

Nathan Shaw had slender shoulders, a threadbare mustache, beady eyes, and a flat, almost hooked nose. Over his black cardigan, he wore a tan trench coat, his pants cinched up by a black leather belt that sported, for a buckle, something huge and country-and-western. The expression on his face was of mild indigestion.

I approached him, moving from bleachers to the field. He turned to me and offered a polite smile.

"I didn't know people still did these things."

"Do you want a button?" I asked.

He scratched his chin, and his eyebrows lifted thoughtfully.

"It would depend on the button."

I handed him one of Hedda's: a pair of stick figures with their arms raised, and underneath, the words "It Takes Two to High-Five."

"Thank you." He affixed the button to his cardigan. "I thought kids didn't want to change the world anymore. If the world happens to change, young people think, so much the better. But you won't stick your neck out for any such thing. I thought you people were too smart for this."

"That's what my father thinks."

"Nothing new under the sun."

"Are you a parent?"

He shook his head.

"Not to anyone here."

"I thought as much," I said. "You don't look like anyone's parent. Haven't seen you at any open houses."

"I wanted to see what this was all about."

"Have you heard about the book?"

He nodded. His face was wide, and his eyes slanted when he grinned.

"There are people who want the book banned. You heard about that?" I asked.

"Something about that."

"You heard about the toxic nerve gas."

"Toxic nerve gas is a failure of the imagination. That may sound old-fashioned, but it's the truth."

"Well, there were threats." I pointed to Navi, who was walking over. "He and I organized the action."

Navi stood beside me. "Are you a reporter?" he asked. "Do you need a quote?"

The man in the cardigan shook his head. Navi waved, then ran back into the crowd. He didn't see the resemblance. No one here did, because no one had bothered to read the book, or even glance at its back cover.

"May I ask you a question?"

"Sure," I said.

"Have you read the book?"

"Haven't quite finished it," I said. "Have you?"

He buried his hands in his coat pockets.

"I recognized you from the photo."

We watched Navi light another bottle rocket. The explosion was followed by someone's shrieking.

"How do you feel, being the cause of all this?" I asked.

"Too old."

I should have asked him why he was here.

"And you came to see this?" I finally asked.

"I happened to be here," said Nathan Shaw, the man for whom my mother had deserted both my father and me on Labor Day 1980, as he stepped off the field. "I'm in town for something."

"A funeral?" I suggested.

"Nice meeting you."

By the time the accordionist and banjo player arrived, kicking into a low-tempo version of "Mack the Knife," the crowd assembled by Navi, having swelled to maybe half the student population by twelve-thirty, seemed ready to disband right before Navi gave his impassioned denouncement of our school, town, nation, and moment in history. Navi introduced me as the person who started the protest earlier this week. This was met with weak applause from Rent-a-Mob.

The walkout succeeded, if only because it was a good excuse to leave school early—much like the walkout we had had two months before, an official event of the graduating class of '98. A point was made, and now, before things dragged out too long, students were ready to clock out and drive to the beach. The members of Rent-a-Mob seemed a little ornery. They had disappointed, pissy looks on their faces—they had driven forty-five minutes from the city for this.

I didn't have the heart for any of it.

"We're storming the principal's office," Navi said after his speech.

"Have you seen Rose?" I asked.

Navi's eyes glazed over. He looked to the ground, his megaphone dangling from his hand by a leather strap.

So I let Navi go. He and the members of Rent-a-Mob proceeded off the soccer field, their angry signs, their two-piece band playing a vaguely Middle Eastern tune, and their inflatable pig in tow. Diapered toddlers and their mothers standing outside the chain-link fences at the very edge of the field, beyond the baseball diamond, watched with interest.

Hedda lagged behind, bent over on the soccer field.

"I have a run in my stocking."

"Sorry."

"Aren't you coming along?"

I shook my head.

"Probably for the best," she said, adjusting her "Miss Police State 1998" sash, which had slipped off when she bent over.

It started to drizzle as I left school for Rose's. I kept my eyes to my scuffed army boots and the pavement below me, watching drops of rain splatter against the sidewalk, feeling them against my neck.

I liked how fresh the air smelled after it rained, and I hoped it would pour. I felt light-headed, the same way I did when I drank coffee on an empty stomach.

I slipped the latch to her backyard and her entrance.

I didn't expect Rose's mother to answer the door. Mrs. Clark was a tall woman whose face was narrow and severe, her hair kept in tight curls. She was in a pair of jeans and a sweatshirt—a change from the lawyer clothes I was used to seeing her in.

"Saul." She opened the door just wide enough to crane her head out.

"Is Rose home?"

"I'm sorry, Saul," she said. "She's not feeling well. I'm off work looking after her."

"Could I see her for a minute?"

"I don't think this is a good time." Mrs. Clark eyed me sharply, and I wondered how much Rose had told her about us. "Sorry," she added softly. She had never especially liked me. I was the one Rose spent nights with when she was supposed to be studying to make good grades. I wondered whether Mrs. Clark would have been so polite if she hadn't known about my mother. For a moment I was glad to be so pitiable.

"I'm sorry, Saul," she repeated, this time as if to say I should go. I heard a toilet flush and the washroom door opening from Rose's room. Mrs. Clark began to close the door. "If you want, I could give her a message."

"Tell her I said hello."

Mrs. Clark nodded and shut the door.

It never really did rain. By early evening, most of the clouds had parted, leaving the sky smeared in bronze.

Jana was at Officer Dale's. Rather than be alone, I went to my father's. The kitchen was still half finished, so we ate dinner outside again. Dad had ordered Chinese food from a pretty decent place in town. I sat in a lawn chair beside Marina, who wore her aviator sunglasses and had two silver butterfly barrettes in her hair. She was drinking a margarita.

Louise came out with a stack of dishes. She placed a blue-checkered cloth on the table and then peeled off the lid from one aluminum container. Steam rose from the beef and broccoli.

"Gord and Nadine said they might come by, though they might be late," she said. She held the shiny side of the lid up so that it reflected the sun.

"Nadine's just come out of the hospital for food poisoning," Marina said. "Maybe she won't be too hungry."

Louise snorted and fit the lid back on the container.

"Douche bag," she said, as she went into the house through the sliding door.

"What's up with her?"

"She's unhappy with me," Marina said. "She thinks I'm stealing your father again. I was out of the shower, and my towel just sort of fell off. A guy gives you a look, and suddenly *you're the whore*."

"You don't want to give someone the wrong idea."

"Men all think the same." Marina was wearing a blue cashmere sweater and a matching skirt with a slit up her right thigh. I felt my throat tighten, my hands balling in jealousy. "Just kidding." She smiled, upper teeth on bottom lip, and squeezed my knee. "I was just trying to get your attention. I wanted to make you jealous."

Marina giggled, her laugh stinging and mocking like a dozen tiny paper cuts. She lit a cigarette, her head falling back against her shoulders as she exhaled. The green polish on her short fingernails was chipped and worn away.

Dad, Richard, and Andreas came outside carrying liter-size beer steins. Richard and Andreas were wearing trucker shirts they must have borrowed from my father. He was in khaki shorts, his hair greased and ponytailed. He seemed surprised to see me.

"Saul." He did a double-take, feigning astonishment. "You've been here an awful lot."

I wanted to hit him very hard.

"I understand your stepmother's remarrying." He sounded as matter-of-fact as he could. But his mouth shriveled, and there was something twitchy in his eyes. I nodded. "Gord spoke to her. How is she?"

"She's happy." I waited for him to say more; he looked as if he wanted to. Instead he mentioned seeing the walkout at school on TV.

"It brought back memories," Dad said, chuckling, his face pink. "Those were glory days." He sat down at the picnic table with Andreas, drinking from his giant mug. "And you organized that? Remarkable. I always suspected I was raising a radical."

"We were protesting the censorship of a book."

"How very noble of you. And the world thanks you."

"I think a healthy participation in political activism is necessary in the life of a student," Louise said, opening a container of hot-and-sour soup.

"The book is called *Baroque-a-Nova*, by Nathan Shaw," I said, in the hope Dad would holler or curse, anything.

My father wasn't terribly tall, and the way he walked, his back all hunched up, made him look shorter. He squinted his silvery eyes and wrinkled his forehead, as if trying to figure a riddle or come up with a punch line. He coughed.

"Well," he said, "the future is in good hands. Next I suppose you'll be picketing me for crimes against humanity or whatever."

"Do you know," Louise said brightly, "that there's a man who wants to rape and shoot Ian?"

"A large man," I corrected.

Dad shook his head. "Those looney tunes think I've done everything to your mother, women, and native people in general."

"Did you see that quiche on TV?" Louise asked. "Did you see it? It was so big. The police pulled the protesters off the bridge, so all there was was that big quiche. It was huge, like forty-eight feet in diameter. It was like an aboveground swimming pool. How much leek would you need for something that big? I mean, you don't have to use leek, but it's for the best—trust me."

Dad was drunk, and once again he was staring at Marina, who was trying to avoid eye contact. A loose, indecent smile spread across his face.

"Well, hello, my pretty," he drawled.

Richard picked up a lawn chair that was leaning against the picnic table and unfolded it beside me.

"Nice duds," Marina said.

"What is the meaning of this idiomatic expression, this 'duds'?"

"We've been conducting, shall we say, a language exchange," Marina said, turning to me, a gleeful expression on her face. "Listen to this: *Deine Oma hat Hängetitten!*"

Richard started snorting like a schoolboy. "Ha, ha. You just said, 'Your grandmother has sagging breasts.'"

"*Mein Leben ist nur ein Haufen Kacke!*"

"'My life is nothing but a pile of crap.'"

"*Sie verkaufen viel Scheissdreck an die Turisten!*"

" 'They sell a lot of shitty junk to the tourists.' "

Marina pointed to his lumberjack shirt.

"Duds."

"Duds," he repeated. "Yeah, is very radical, right?" he said, admiring his shirt. We nodded. "I am feeling, like, comfortable in this country. I believe the Canadian soul is to be found in absence and distance, in its native traditions."

"You mean like totem poles?" Marina said. "I suppose we are in the Pacific Northwest. Or do Canadians call this area the Southwest?"

I gave her a dirty look.

"I want to ask you, Saul," Richard said, touching my hand, "about your native heritage, your mother. Quickly, because I do not have very much time. I have finished speaking to your father and this friend, the pedal-steel player, this Gordon. Now, before I return to Germany, I must speak to you. Tomorrow is good, yeah?"

"I don't think so." There was already my mother's involuntary valediction, and of course my father's idiotic rebuttal. My father, who said nothing to me, nothing to Jana, practically spewing his life when a camera was turned on him.

"Then Sunday," Richard said. "Urethra Franklin leaves for Japan on Sunday, and I must follow shortly thereafter."

"I'd rather not."

"Do I frighten you?" he said. His voice rose again, sharp and high, and the beer in his hand trembled. "Does my accent bewilder you? Do you find my manner brusque and iconoclastic?"

"Excuse me?"

"Why do you insist on jeopardizing my career? Why do you resist me?"

"Richard, can you lay off?" Marina said. "Saul is telling you he's no media whore."

Dad grunted.

Richard took a sip from his beer, then wiped a line of foam from his upper lip. He stood up from his lawn chair and placed his hand on my father's back. Dad's flannel shirt was a little too small for Richard around the shoulders, but he still looked better in it than my father.

"Please, Ian, talk to your son."

"Richard," Dad said, "all I ever do is talk."

The arrangements had been made. The body of my mother was expected to arrive on Saturday. There was to be a viewing Sunday, a Catholic funeral and burial Monday. The speeches would be given Sunday, since Catholic services were more formal— long-winded and impersonal, Dad said, little more than regular Masses with coffins. Already, I was told, there were people in town from Toronto and New York and San Francisco, touring-band members, backup singers, and record people from the days of the St. Pierres—friends of my parents' whom my father had lost touch with in the eighteen years since my mother's disappearance. And more to come.

Gord and Nadine arrived. He passed by me, clapping a hand on my shoulder. He was wearing an old pair of denim flares and a Captain Beefheart T-shirt. He smiled and pulled me into a head-lock. I tensed up in his grip and he let me go. He asked how I was doing, and I nodded senselessly.

Nadine looked pale in a pair of white cutoffs and a pink sleeveless shirt, her hair tied into two pigtails. She still wore her hospital bracelet.

"How are you feeling?" Marina asked, nibbling on a piece of honey-and-garlic spare rib.

"Terrible," Nadine said. "Simply miserable."

"It was only a little food poisoning," Gord said.

"Says you," Nadine said. She was looking at her fingernails. "One of the doctors was about this close to amputating a leg."

"That never happened, Nadine."

"I was at death's door."

"Not true."

"You have no clue. I don't think you even tried to understand how I felt lying in the hospital all alone."

"Alone? I was with you the whole time."

"I was alone, *Gord*—metaphorically—because no one knew how I felt."

"Sometimes I don't understand a word you're saying."

"They said I was this close to needing a liver transplant."

Dad came out of the house with his old reel-to-reel tape player. He put the machine on the picnic table and spooled a tape with "Labor Day 1980" marked on it, just as he had promised Richard. We listened to my mother's recorded voice here, in my father's backyard, for the second time this week. There was applause and then we heard the opening chords to "Great Slave Lake," the first song on the St. Pierres' fifth and final album, *Broken Heart's Daydream*:

> *I want to ask you something before you wake*
> *I've been thinking how the summer must end*
> *Will our love fade like the sun against Great Slave Lake?*
> *Will our love fade like the sun against Great Slave Lake?*

At the farm I trace the days you're in the city
Against the dew on the windowpanes
Will our love fade like the sun against Great Slave Lake?
Will our love fade like the sun against Great Slave Lake?

I feel like I'm losing time
Mired in the crickets' chime
Until I feel your breath against my cheek
Let us sleep in an embrace
Let me dream of your sweet face
How wonderful to make true
This song of love I sing to you

Our love will rise again
Like the sun against Great Slave Lake
Our love will rise again
Like the sun against Great Slave Lake

"Yeah, this suicide made everything so very disorganized. When we arrived in Bangkok, we tried ringing her," Richard said, "but she didn't pick up her phone. She lived in Potpang." He shook his head. "Not a nice area. We asked her neighbors in the housing complex about her, but they knew nothing of this woman—only that she was polite and kind, but remained alone. We tried to find the church where she did her missionary work, but a taxi driver took us to a Pizza Hut and brandished a knife in our faces when we protested. We decided to knock at her door. We didn't expect her to react in such a way when we found her, that she would be so, so *unreasonable.*"

"And you expected what?" I asked.

"What happened was lamentable," Richard said, sounding defensive and irritated, "but I acted as would a journalist."

"Do you think she moved to Thailand because she wanted you to find her?"

Richard said nothing.

Dad scratched the back of his neck, his eyes soft and far away, apparently lost in the music.

"Christ," Louise said, "I was seven when this recording was made. I'm surprised the tape sounds as good as it does."

Marina stood by the reel-to-reel.

"I think seventies stereo technology is cooler," she said. "It was the age of beanbags and lava lamps, when stereos were meant to be in the basement. These days you get stereos in little components, and they're always black or gray. They're so boring. The designs were sleeker back then. The knobs were bigger."

"Slut," Louise said.

The next few songs were from *Bushmills Threnody* and the second album, *Prairie Winds.* Then the later stuff. The applause recorded was noticeably less enthusiastic for the songs from the last two albums. They had sold poorly, in spite of my father's best efforts to give listeners what they wanted.

When she performed, my mother would utter not a single word to the audience. From all accounts, she stood there completely still, a small woman with eyes like dark thoughts.

Gord smiled, his horsey, gummy mouth open wide, and tapped his foot along to the music.

Nadine found nail clippers in her purse and started clipping her toenails at the picnic table.

Richard and Andreas held their beer steins against their chests, their heads drooping solemnly.

Louise sat next to Dad, her mouth in a hard, unforgiving frown, glaring at Marina.

Marina was in the lawn chair beside me. She seemed upset. Her arms were crossed, her eyes were clear and empty, and her mouth twitched indignantly.

The early-evening sun fell upon us, warm, forgiving, absent-minded.

We heard the sound of a sprinkler in the next yard, whisking in the air, water splattering.

The air smelled like mown grass.

I sat in the lawn chair with my ankles crossed underneath, blood rushing to my ears. I pitied my father. He didn't say anything. He drank his beer and listened to the cracks and breaths of my mother's voice, to the Moog synthesizer's transistor-driven keening, to Gord's pedal-steel sweetly gliding toward a major-seven chord, to his own chiming twelve-string. He let out a little groan after each song, every one of them leading closer to the show's end. I would have let my memory fail.

"What's your problem?" Marina asked after the recording had ended. Dad had gone inside, to return the tape to his closet.

"Your little slutty ass," Louise said, stacking the dirty dishes.

"Bite me."

"At least I'm not named after a place where they store boats."

"Cunt."

"Home away from home for wayward sailors."

"Fuckface."

"The last stop for solitary seamen, sinking their anchors."

"A fifty-year-old man wanting to fuck you doesn't mean more than it does. It just is what it is."

"I think you're jealous," Louise said.

"Why would I be jealous of you? What do you have that I'd want?"

"A father. A trust fund. A happy childhood."

Marina said nothing, her eyes still, looking past the back fence to the highway.

Louise picked up the pile of dishes as if to leave for the kitchen. Then she put them back on the table.

"You need male attention so badly that you'll fuck anyone between the ages of fifty and eighteen," she said.

We all sat there silently until Dad came back out, wearing a pair of sunglasses.

"The funeral's Monday, folks," he said. He turned to Louise. "What's your damage?"

Louise, her hand covering her mouth, disappeared into the house with the dishes. We heard the faucet running.

"I try to tell her to stop," Dad said, nodding toward ever-helpful Louise, "but the girl can't help herself."

Marina rolled down the window and rested her arm against the door. Even now, after the sun had set, the air and the pavement felt warm. The streetlights along Trunk Road buzzed prematurely, pale white in the orange twilight, as the days had grown more reluctant to give way to darkness.

"I can understand why you want to get out of here," Marina said quietly.

"How do you know I want to leave?"

"Who would want to stay?" she asked impatiently. "What are you waiting for?"

Maybe she had been trying to hit on my father. Maybe she was hurt and fucked up, and she acted in certain ways to get the attention of men. I was willing to overlook that. I wanted her that badly.

We turned onto the highway at Trunk Road and moved south.

"Where are you taking me?"

We drove through Tsawwassen, past the ferries that led to Vancouver Island, then on a side road flanked by cow pastures and tulip fields and cherry orchards until we reached a small public beach, just off a new condominium development. We parked in the empty lot, by a dune overlooking the beach and the ocean. I cut the engine. I could hear myself breathe.

"This is where you take your girlfriend?" she asked.

I nodded.

She looked at me, a stern expression on her face. Then she moved toward me, holding my stare. I dropped my hand against her hip and ran it up, against soft flesh and rib bone, up until I felt her bra. I tried not to burp when I kissed her; we ended up banging teeth instead. I tasted the cigarette smoke on her breath. The corners of her mouth lifted into a smile, then fell. I kissed her again—slowly, wetly, and well.

"I think," she said, "everyone deserves a second chance."

"Thank you," I said. "Thank you very much."

I sat there, my chest hollowing, feeling good about the world. Every moment should be like this—one that could be relived, rehearsed, and consumed over and over again, prepared for and wanly imagined.

"Do you like my barrettes?" She pointed to the shiny butterflies in her hair.

I nodded. I thought she had said something else.

She laughed.

I sat there thinking I should quit now. We moved to the back, climbing over the emergency brake, and undressed beneath a blanket my dad kept folded above the backseat, beside the first-aid kit and the rear stereo speakers. I felt Marina's tongue flicking between my teeth, her short fingernails with their cracked green polish along my back. I felt her stomach. I was hard and Marina straddled me between her legs and I could smell the sea on her skin.

SATURDAY

We were on our way to the funeral home on the far side of town, the windshield wipers of Dad's car squeaking as they swept off the rain, which fell in fine pellets. He let me tag along, Louise on the passenger side, me in the back, where I had ended up the night before. I didn't know why Louise bothered to come, why she needed to drape herself around my father at this time. Not that there was an especially good time for any of this. Dad was dressing better, even respectably. Maybe he felt the clothes suited the occasion, or maybe he was hoping to impress. All this week he had shaved regularly, worn clean shirts tucked into dark corduroys or jeans. Yet the effort and preening didn't suit his threadbare soul. He looked sad.

"So I read this book by this Nathan Shaw guy, the one that was banned at Saul's school," Louise said. "I've been meaning to read it for a while. It was nominated for an award back in the seventies, an award given by an island, one of those Island Council Association something awards that make you think of pregnant women in flares and kerchiefs." She lowered her voice: "It's about her, isn't it, Ian? It's about Helena."

Dad shrugged and mumbled. "She was supposed to have left with him. A fling. That's what I understood."

"Not that it's a bad book, it's all right. It's a quick read. A first novel by any definition. Okay, sometimes Mr. Shaw goes off on tangents, but he has a lot of metaphors for crying—like thirty or forty of them. I really can't say it's worth public outcry—you know, toxic nerve gas threats. The public does what it sees fit."

"Just like fickle women."

Louise kept running her mouth. She was nervous because Dad and I weren't saying much. She mentioned her screenplay. She suggested Dad take a vacation after the funeral, then glanced at him for a reaction and out the window, her tiny head ping-ponging back and forth. My dad looked straight ahead, silently, neither menacing nor malicious, nothing like the man who'd once seethed, and plotted against Jana and me at the dinner table, yelling at her for spending, at me for general turpitude. Today he lacked conviction. He looked the way he did sitting alone in the kitchen, strumming a guitar, quietly rhyming words to G chords, a pen and notepad on the table, before losing it, realizing there would be no one to sing whatever he wrote in any event, putting his guitar carefully back into its case, replacing it on the top shelf of his closet.

Dad looking slightly pissed off, knuckles taut on the steering wheel, staring ahead with a hollowed-out expression, cross-eyed in grief.

We pulled into the Silver and Gold Motor Inn. A man in a priest's collar stood in the parking lot. He stepped over a puddle to approach us.

"Ian St. Pierre?" he asked. He carried his height awkwardly, had a long neck, and hips that widened below his waist, like a woman's.

"Father Felix?"

They shook hands. The priest got into the backseat, next to me.

"Father Felix," Dad explained, "worked with Leni in Thailand. The two of them helped the poor."

"She was a kind woman," Father Felix said. "She was at the parish before me—showed me the ropes, really. I was new."

"I spoke to Felix after your mother died," Dad said. "He was so kind to deal with the people at the embassy and escort the body home."

"I suggested it. Didn't want to miss her funeral. If there was anything I could do, could've done, you know."

Felix's eyes fell on me, small blue gumdrops on his saucer-of-milk face—a twenty-year-old face, not a day older. He wore his hair swept sideways, with apparently liberal amounts of hairspray, so it held solid and unnaturally, as if he had an ugly wig. His chubby neck chafed in his collar.

Louise smiled at him. "May I ask you a question?"

"You were wondering about my age?"

"I'm sorry," she said. "I meant to be subtle."

"Oh, no. I get it all the time. I started young and I look younger, but I've been with the Church almost ten years." He chuckled. "It puts some people off at first, so I go out of my way to explain. I received the call when I was eighteen."

"That sounds pretty eager."

Father Felix considered this, then laughed politely.

"I'd imagine eighteen-year-olds would have other things on their minds besides God," Louise said.

"I guess. But I wasn't too different. I lusted," he said, chuckling nervously in recollection. "Then I received the call."

Louise looked amused. "What was that like? Did you hear the voice of God?"

"No, not exactly. The Virgin Mary appeared at the foot of my bed when I was in my senior year of high school. It was a shocking experience, something I was completely unprepared for. Before then, you couldn't say I was terribly concerned about religion."

"You had a religious epiphany. Just like Helena St. Pierre." Louise said this a little sourly, with a hint of mockery that Father Felix chose to ignore.

"She was a sweet woman."

"Mary or Helena St. Pierre?"

"Both."

We drove past an older man watering his lawn amid ceramic ornaments and a miniature windmill. A wire fence separated the cemetery from the rest of the neighborhood. Pink and gray marble headstones dotted one side of a patchy lawn, the other side reserved for nameplates flat on the ground. The bouquets and flower arrangements on both sides were matted down by the rain.

The parking lot covered the area between a mausoleum, a stone building with stained-glass French windows, framed by hedges, and an office. We parked next to a white pickup with a small orange crane in its bed and went along a tiled path through a garden, past a pond and two park benches, the chapel, in a white-washed complex with two steep black roofs. Once inside the chapel, we walked down a long hallway lined with octagonal windows. At every window was a table with a floral arrangement and a box of tissues. At the end of the hall was the office, which was soft and carpeted like a doctor's, only with more tissues. The receptionist asked us to sit, then picked up a phone. She was a trim woman, probably in her thirties, wearing a summer blouse and sandals. She put down the phone and told us someone would be talking to us shortly. I sat in a stiff leather armchair next to a water cooler, flipping through the *Times* and *Entertainment Weekly*s fanned across a glass-topped coffee table, opposite a portrait of a serious-looking man in a blue suit. Dad, hands in his pants pockets, paced in a circle.

A man in a dark suit appeared. He had a narrow face, a hairline that dropped far back, and a bushy, graying mustache. He shook our hands with a firm, clammy grip. He looked like a direct descendant of the man in the portrait. "I'm Mr. Dirk," he said. "Follow me." He led us down another hall until we reached the room where the viewing would be held, the chapel. We entered from the rear entrance, through a dimly lit reception area with low-slung chairs and a long table next to two heavy doors. It was a cream-colored room, not so big, the pews backed with maroon cushions. Stale light fell through the skylights in the peaked maple ceiling. There was a lectern up front. Next to it, the wheels of a coffin had left grooves in the salmon-pink plush carpet. The room smelled like cedar oil.

Louise tugged Dad's denim shirtsleeve.

"This is where the funeral's being conducted?" she asked.

"Just the viewing," Dad said, mumbling. He looked distracted, slouching even further, as if he were counting with his hands in his pockets. "The funeral's Monday, at a church."

"We understand this might be an unusual case," the funeral director said. "We've been taking calls from the press ourselves—discreetly, of course." My father nodded. "Should we discuss the schedule of the viewing and burial here or in my office?"

"Of course," Dad said. Then, after a timid gulp, "Once I see her body."

"Perhaps we might address more immediate concerns. There is, for instance, the issue of the music to be played. Our organist is very talented—he used to do weddings and arena sporting events before they took to using tapes. Then there are the flower arrangements and method of payment, as well."

Dad persisted. The smile on the funeral director's face seemed to peel away, his voice trailing off. The body was not yet prepared for viewing, he explained.

"I think it would be better for me if I saw her," Dad said.

"Can't you wait?" I asked.

He ignored me. It was blood lust, I thought.

"Honestly," Mr. Dirk said finally, his voice sharper, "she's a mess." Dad kept his eyes on the funeral director until, with a tired smirk, he relented. They disappeared through a side exit.

Father Felix stood near a pew, inspecting the cushions.

"I was just thinking," he told me, a big smile on his face, "how you must be the very same age I was when I joined the Church."

"Oh." I nodded politely. I pictured myself in black, saying prayers and giving Communion, and felt nervous as hell.

"Enjoy yourself now, Saul. You'll regret it otherwise." He sighed wistfully. "It was certainly a difficult time in my life. I had trouble keeping my mind on things."

"Hormones."

"I remember my first vision of Mary. She was in a halter top and fishnets. A fine-looking young woman. Very healthy. Robust."

Louise was standing at the lectern in a flower-print blouse and shorts, leaning against it. There were padded benches on either side behind the lectern, and flags.

"What do you do in Thailand, Father Felix?" she asked.

"We run a home for the kids—young women, mostly. There are a lot of orphans in Bangkok. There's a choir."

"And were you close to Helena?"

Father Felix's face went red. He struggled to get out a word.

"I was shy around her, I must admit," he said with hesitation. "I suppose I'm generally a shy person. I admired her. We did some work together in the country, where they don't treat children well, especially girls."

"They sell their daughters," Louise said.

Father Felix sighed again. "I'm afraid they do."

I stared up at the overcast sky, brown and impenetrable, through the skylights. This whole place was creepy.

The night before, I had dreamt about my mother for the first time since the suicide. I saw her entering my father's backyard, sliding open the glass door, Dad beside the grill in an apron, wiping his brow with the inside of his forearm, Marina and Louise, Jana and Rose at the picnic table. She sat down and ate with us. We were surprised to see her, but no one said a word to her. We just watched her eat and eat. All she did in my dream was eat. I forgot what happened next. I didn't remember what she looked like in my dream, or whether I even said anything to her. I woke up and there was a moment before I realized I had been dreaming. My heart filled that instant, before it returned to normal.

I imagined my mother's body lying in another room on a slab of stainless steel, wrapped in plastic.

"Your father's been very generous," Father Felix was saying. "He paid my way here, provided for my lodging. You must thank him again for me."

"Sure." And I wondered how my father had suddenly become so generous. He usually had his reasons. To impress, to appease, to apologize. I felt a shudder run down my neck and ripple through my spine to my knees.

"Are you a friend of Saul's?" Father Felix asked Louise.

"I'm a friend of Ian's," she said, looking at me with her head bowed. Her mouth was tight and small.

Father Felix nodded, as if to say he understood.

I sat down and rested my head against the back of the pew ahead of me.

"You look like you're praying," Louise said.

I started banging my head against the pew.

"Did she speak about me?"

Father Felix rubbed his eyes with his thumb and forefinger as though he was groggy or had allergies. "Saul, she was very troubled."

"What was my mother like, Father Felix?" I asked.

She was in another room, a corpse.

It is one dramatic exit after another, departures appropriate for someone who actively seeks excitement, a woman who has forsaken her clothes for an Introduction to Life Drawing, in public, in front of photographers, paper and charcoal extra, a black-eyed waif hard-wired for impulsiveness. That's why she beats the men off with a stick, even putting your dad into fits of chain-smoking sullenness, his neck exposed, a frown on his wretched face. As much as he philanders and bosses and cajoles her, he is whipped. Whatever hurt he doles out to her, enough pain to force her away from the world, she returns tenfold in her silence. She is moody and terrified to step onstage, quickly slighted and spiteful in her small-boned way. Fame aggravates every one of her tics. It makes her more alluring, more solitary, more pitiful, more difficult, more easily bored. With her voice, she bestows on the music, the vapid mushy folk, its shadows, its low-riding heart.

Say your mother's been hearing things, like a radio crossed between two stations, the steel twang of a blues weeper cutting into the knuckled vowels of three Scotsmen debating federalism on the AM band. The drugs were making her fat, so she stopped using them, and then they returned, louder and even more urgent, like a busload of children stalled in the snow.

Once she lets go, she finds herself relieved. She sits in the dark and listens to her brain humming. She sleeps with them talking to her.

She doesn't intend to sing the encore. Instead, she speeds past security people and the opening band watching *That's Incredible!* and drinking white wine that smells like nail polish remover, through basement corridors, her cowboy boots clacking down a fire escape and out into the summer night. They wait for her onstage for ten minutes, the audience responding with heavier applause, stamping their feet on the floor. Dad runs backstage and yells at everyone. An assistant sent to her dressing room comes back with no Leni. Dad rolls his eyes and proceeds to inform all present that their value has plummeted below their weight in pigeon shit.

The band plays an unrehearsed version of "Peter Gunn," with an extended drum break, to kill time. The crowd sounds pissy. Someone throws a quarter at the band, welting Gord on the forehead—the punk culture, the yobs dragging us into the sewer once and for all, in the process making music like the St. Pierres' sound overproduced and glossy, a landing zone for derision.

The stage is as dark as a witch's cauldron, the room stewing with humidity, swelling with idle sweat. A single spotlight rests on a microphone in the middle of the stage. Dad turns to Jana in her dashiki, her hands folded over her chest. "You know where she is, don't you?" he asks. "Tell me," he screams. Jana, who is by then secretly, desperately in love with him, denies everything.

Say your mother wants less of this world. Say she wants it to collapse into her pocket. She wants less of her husband, his clinging and abuse, his schedules and bitter words. It would be impossible to stop the tour, for them to divorce and skulk out of courtrooms with their collars turned up, for child custody to be established, bank accounts located and sorted and halved. In spite of her protests, he has carried on as if they had no choice about the tour, the radio interviews and autograph sessions, as if they were simply unable to walk away from it all. So she calls an old boyfriend—the dependable one, who never forgot her in his heart—to pick her up, mid-tour, to run off with her and drive his rental car to the airport. Eventually she'll cut him loose, too.

Ian steps onto the stage on Labor Day 1980, and walks toward the spotlight to make an announcement. The crowd cackles, expecting Helena St. Pierre. He turns back without saying a word and tells the stage manager to turn on the lights—show's over.

I watched Father Felix in the chapel, a wedge of light falling like a hand onto his shoulder as he stood underneath a skylight. He started to answer my question when Dad returned from the same side entrance from which he'd left. He looked pale, his face sour. Mr. Dirk extended a handkerchief to him, pressed and silk, as red as a valentine. Dad took it. Louise started to say something, but Dad waved her off with his borrowed hanky. He told her to shut up. Dad wiped a thin white string of puke from his chin, then sat next to me, his head rocking back and forth, mouth open, my forehead pressed against the pew, exhausted, conscious, the two of us, father and son.

A large woman in a dull brown apron stood behind the counter of the doughnut shop in front of the glazes and almond powders and pink sprinkles being offered. She looked familiar and smiled at me as I walked in. She had a small upturned nose and was fat, her hands ashen in clear plastic gloves, holding a pair of kitchen tongs.

"How are you?" she asked.

"I'm fine."

"And how is your stepmother?"

"Jana's fine."

"And how is your father?"

"My father's fine."

"Your father should be shot like the dog he is."

The doughnut shop was in the strip mall, with its flat and khaki stucco exteriors, and its shopping carts neatly slotted together beside shrubbed traffic islands, three blocks off the gentrified main drag. This was the unpopular strip mall—the one with the thrift store and fabric warehouse. Across the street was a newer development with two coffeehouses and a shop devoted to fancy soaps. The new mall bought into a West Coast lifestyle talked about in magazines, where people my parents' age, who ended up as lawyers and computer executives and therapists, took tai chi classes and purchased Mexican hand-blown glass. My parents were among the few people of their generation who had chosen not to settle down and become respectable. They were failures.

Marina was waiting for me at the table by the window, stirring her coffee with a red plastic stick. In front of her on her tray, sitting on a square piece of wax paper, were glazed chocolate doughnut holes.

Two white men in flannel shirts and steel-toed boots sat in the booth next to us, reading their sports pages and eyeing Marina, sneering at me for whatever reason—who knows. On account that I was a skinny, ethnic boy with greasy hair, in my Nomeansno

T-shirt and my combat pants, not quite out of high school, from a broken home. There was craziness in my family, from both sides. It ran through my veins like the cars speeding along the highway at night. Craziness and hormones. A Muzak version of a Clash song was playing in the shop, Marina, not really thinking, tapping a fingernail, newly painted in silver sparkle, against the yellow tabletop to the beat. I felt sort of nervous and sort of bad, a little cocky because I could still taste her skin, mostly anxious because the taste was faint.

I popped a doughnut hole in my mouth.

"What is your fascination with doughnuts?" she asked.

"The typical fascination."

She laughed again.

She drank her creamed coffee, her teeth resting on her bottom lip as she smiled, her lips a brick, earthy red—the color of a dried wound.

I felt like crying. "Rose likes doughnut holes, too."

"Oh. How is your girlfriend?"

"She hasn't been returning my calls."

Doughnuts were among the first things Rose would swear off when she decided to lose weight. She would diet, and swim two hours a day, but her metabolism was awful and she just wouldn't get any thinner. I hated seeing her diet. I pictured her at school eating her alfalfa on whole-wheat. It made me feel like crying.

Marina tucked a strand of hair behind her ear, her mouth in a pained expression.

"My mom's a psychic, you know that?"

I shook my head.

"A one-nine-hundred-number type who works out of her house, at her kitchen table. She spends her evenings drinking Tom

Collinses with dates she meets through newspaper ads and services. She says it's the easiest way to meet nice men. One night when I was twelve, after my stepfather had run out, she put pictures of three men on the kitchen table. 'I have it narrowed down to these three,' she told me. 'You decide.'"

"Last night," I felt compelled to say, "was my fault."

She blushed. "You're sweet," she said, laughing, "to take the blame."

Marina in pigtails, wearing pearl earrings and stringy rubber bracelets, in a blue tank top and matching skirt. She nodded and made a violin-bowing motion in the air. I didn't know exactly what she meant by that, whether she was making fun of me or sympathizing. There lay the attraction.

She finished her coffee and suggested we leave.

"Your father should be shot like the dog he is," the woman behind the counter repeated.

I still couldn't place her, with her chubby fingers and her highlighted sandy-brown hair. She was stupid-looking, like Nadine almost, stupid and loud and opinionated. She must have been a fan.

"Who are you?" I asked. Marina hung by my side, ready to go.

"You don't remember me?"

I said I didn't.

"I haven't seen you in years, since you were a tiny infant. But all this time I've been watching you."

We heard banging outside, and turned to see Anders rapping against the plate-glass window. He held a bouquet of white daisies, bright against his dusky face.

"I called the school," he said. "They won't teach his filthy book anymore."

"Not you again." The doughnut lady left her spot at the counter. "I told you to buzz off."

"The lies they tell about you," Anders yelled.

"Go," she said from the doorway. "I have work to do."

The corners of Anders's mouth turned back. He sprinted away, dropping his daisies as he ran. She squatted to pick up the flowers, then threw them in a trashcan inside.

Marina and I left the shop. In the parking lot, kids on mountain bikes, ten-year-olds in dusty baseball uniforms, whipped by us, one hand on their handlebars, orange and purple Mr. Freezes in the other.

Marina and I went to the thrift store occupying the space that was once a supermarket. The windows took up its face, and the high ceiling sloped up at the middle. Crockery and appliances—once white blenders, dented toaster ovens with glass doors filmy from grease—were off to the side. We entered next to shelves of used Harlequins, their spines cracked white, with men's and women's wear to the left, shoes and children's clothes at the back. A young Indian woman was working the only register open, ringing in a pair of platform shoes for a purple-haired girl, who held a skateboard at her hip.

I watched Marina flipping through outfits, the wire coat hangers and their plastic clips clicking as she did. When she found something promising, she folded it over her forearm.

She looked up at me and smiled.

"I didn't expect to be here this long. I pack lightly."

The dressing room doors were like those of a saloon in a western. I waited outside as she changed, and held on to her coat hangers. I could see her bare shoulders, and her skirt falling to her ankles and bunching on the floor.

She appeared in a black suit jacket with shoulder pads and a white polka-dot collar.

"Too sexy," she said.

She came out in two other dark dresses before I realized that she was dressing for a funeral.

"Sometimes I think my breasts are a fucking curse," she said. She cupped them in her hands and studied them, a pleasantly surprised look on her face. "I take that back."

I watched Marina undress again later that afternoon, though this time in my old room. She unbuttoned her skirt and folded it on a chair, over which she placed her bra, black, undone at the front.

We heard the front door open and close, then the floorboards creak, the sound of someone stepping to the kitchen.

I sat on the cot. The curtains had yet to be drawn. I could see the neighbors' yard over Marina's shoulder. They never turned off their sprinkler in the summer. They were terrible, terrible people, I decided.

We heard Louise asking if anyone was home.

Marina stood in front of me, her body lined in daylight.

It wasn't illegal, what we were doing. I was eighteen years old and consenting—in a big way. And these were the suburbs, after all. She moved two steps toward me, demurely, a microscopic smile on her face, her eyes bright like she was thinking about a joke she'd just heard, the one Freud told comparing marriage to an umbrella—sooner or later you take a cab. She stood before me, her knees scraping against mine, allowing me to inspect her, to admire her. I examined her for imperfections, scrupulously, like a jeweler, handling her with the tips of my thumb and forefinger. I looked for scars, purple blotches on an inner thigh, pale white lines from surgery, butterfly-shaped moles. I didn't find any.

I told her I loved her.

She shook her head.

I traced a fingernail from above her pussy, up her waist to the bone between her breasts. She took my cock with her thumb and index finger and gave it a couple of tugs, a frisky look on her face.

"Lie down," I said.

"The magic word is what."

"What." I paused. "Please."

She smiled and sat down at the edge of the cot. I leaned into her, her breath against my neck, and we were horizontal. She swung her feet onto the bed, her knees slightly raised.

I slipped down until I was between her legs, my hands on her hips. I kissed her stomach and her inner thighs. I ran my tongue along the outer lips of her pussy, then split them open with my fingers, moved my tongue up and down until I found her clitoris. Her legs shuddered. I stopped.

"I haven't done this before."

"Take your time," she said, in a whisper. She giggled, tickled. "Start slow, regularly, then, um, you know, pick up the pace."

We found Louise in the living room, smoking cloves and typing away at her laptop. Two airplane bottles of rum sat on the coffee table, one empty. She raised a hand at us, with almost regal disinterest, but continued typing. Once she finished whatever she was typing, she looked up, surprised to see us.

"Oh, there you are," she said. "Did you just get in?"

"Where's Ian?" Marina sat down next to her on the leather couch and placed her feet on the hassock.

"He wanted to talk to Father Felix. There was estate stuff that needed to be settled." She tapped her clove against Dad's ashtray, a beer bottle melted so it looked like a life raft. She said, still staring into the screen, "He wanted some time by himself."

"I see."

"Sometimes I think love is an emotion best felt alone." Louise laughed, maybe a little too hard, as if to say she was sorry. "What did you do today?"

"I bought a funeral dress with Saul. It's really cute. If you want, I can show it to you later."

"Okay."

"Would it be okay if we made up?"

"Sure. Do you want to hear a bit of my screenplay?" Louise asked.

Marina nodded.

"'Exterior, night. Enter Margaret, in a pale-blue suit dress cut above the knee, from an airplane. She is greeted by Fidel Castro.'"

The doorbell rang.

I went to get the door, leaving the two of them in the living room.

Richard and Andreas were standing there.

Richard's eye was black. He said he'd been looking for me.

"Good news. Urethra Franklin would like to meet you. I spoke to Rob this morning about you, and he would like to propose a creative venture. We're late for the show. We may have already missed it."

"What happened to your eye?"

"Oh," he said, and turned to Andreas, who was still in his black leather vest, his arms folded. "Your father hit me. We had a disagreement. But now, now everything is good."

We were on our way to the city, to the Franklin concert. Our car was stuck in traffic, because of an accident. Marina rolled down the window in the back. She and Louise were yelling at each other in the backseat, with Andreas stuck in the middle, looking on gamely. Richard sat in front, inspecting his eye in the vanity mirror.

"The band wants to meet you," he said. "I've described you to them, mentioned your resemblance. They're intrigued, this is natural. They want to extend their condolences. Do you sing?"

The thought made me giggle. I had no musical ability whatsoever. My father's efforts to teach me guitar had ended badly, with my fingers raw and my feelings hurt. I was eleven and had wanted to learn—back then I still admired my father and his porky, callused fingers. I couldn't sing.

"They think they can turn you into a recording star. Their new single is not doing so well. They want your voice on a remixed version."

I asked Richard why my father had hit him.

"He thinks I have been asking too much of him. I interviewed him again this afternoon, and he thinks my questions are impolite. I said I needed total disclosure. He said our cash arrangement did not specify total disclosure."

"Cash arrangement?"

"Yes, a sum was exchanged in return for exclusive information, including his interview." Richard turned off the vanity mirror light and flipped up the sun visor. His long legs were pushed against the glove compartment. "You notice I haven't asked to speak to you today."

I nodded, figuring this to be the windfall my father came upon that allowed him to pay for his house renovations, the burial costs. Yet something remained unsettled. I felt dizzy.

Richard chuckled, then removed an envelope from his jacket pocket. "I have decided to let you come to me."

I opened Richard's envelope. Inside was a cashier's cheque for ten thousand dollars. I held it up, so that I could see it in the halogen white lights of the cars behind us.

"Keep it," Richard said. "Let me know your decision by tomorrow—no, Monday."

Meanwhile Louise had decided, while we listened to Neil Young's *Rust Never Sleeps*, that rock and roll had indeed died.

"But it's always been an art form that had a low originality quotient," Marina was arguing, "sprung from primeval longing. It follows a long-standing tradition of white guys wishing they were black. British guys really wishing they were sharecroppers."

"I guess what I mean is that rock and roll is no longer a mass movement, the sound track to large-scale opposition," Louise said. "It's come to an end, the fire-sale point of rock and roll's history. What we have instead is cannibalism in pop music. Bands used to steal guitar licks off their albums. Now they - sample them, they delete vocal tracks and punch in drum tracks and loop bass lines. They settle lawsuits over copyright infringements."

"My stepbrother's obsession in high school was with live albums," Marina said. "*Live at Leeds, The Song Remains the Same, After the Flood, Live Rust, Loco Live, Live at Winterland, Frampton Comes Alive*. Bootlegs galore. He didn't even go to any concerts, on account of some phobia or another, but he had to have the live albums. Every day I'd walk past his room and hear the roar of the crowd.

"Strange guy, my stepbrother," she added. "He died, drowned in the bathtub, when I was fourteen, two years after his dad divorced my mom."

"Christ, you never told me that," Louise said. "What happened?"

"He was testing scuba gear."

We were late. By the time we got into the city and to the eastside stadium, we had missed the performance. Not that I minded, but Richard and Andreas needed footage from the show for a segment about the Canadian tour. We parked the car behind the stadium, watching girls and older men in Urethra Franklin T-shirts and Urethra Franklin hemp bracelets stream out of the stadium, past booths with information on reproductive rights and logging treaties.

Richard got out and went to an entrance, where he talked to a woman who held a clipboard against her chest. She followed him to the car.

When they reached the car, she crouched to my window, a laminated ID card dangling from her neck. She seemed to recognize me. I turned off the radio.

"We've been waiting for you," she said.

"Come," Richard said, "we are going backstage."

"How many of you are there?" the woman asked him.

"Four."

"Fine." She removed four laminates from her clipboard. "Let's go."

The woman told me she was a big fan, just that, as if I'd done something special. She introduced herself and told me she was a backstage assistant, but I forgot her name immediately—I was getting good at that. We followed her along the lot to a fenced area behind the building where the tour buses were parked. She nodded at two security guards as we passed the rear entrance. The backstage area was all concrete and ugly piping, lent a dull pallor by fluorescent lights.

"They play hockey here, yeah?" Richard asked. "They play curling here, do they not?"

On the stage, cables were being slung around the thick shoulders of men in overalls, and speakers rolled along on carts.

There were couches against the walls, and tables set up for a buffet and bar. There were musicians, a guy holding drumsticks with a towel around his neck, and a skinny albino guy in a hard hat with tattoos running down his arms, milling around the open bar, eating crackers and drinking from plastic cups. Beside them were the Franklins' friends, the quiche-makers.

Richard wanted to know where Urethra Franklin was. The assistant pointed to a door at the far end of the room. Richard excused himself. He wanted to speak to the band alone first.

There was the radio personality from the press conference camped beside the oyster bar.

Ramona the VJ was sitting on a canvas folding chair. She was sipping from a bottle of water.

"Oh, look," Marina said. "There's our friend, the French tart."

"Hey, pedal pushers," Louise said, giggling. "Nice."

"What a fashion trendsetter."

"Or does she prefer the term 'capri pants'?"

"My goodness, it's the young cameraman," Ramona said. "And look"—she nodded at Marina—"you've brought your mother again. How is it you are here? You win a contest, eh? Meet the band. You save your bottle caps?"

The assistant put her hand on my elbow.

"He's a guest of honor. May I introduce to you Helena St. Pierre's son, Saul. Saul St. Pierre."

"I didn't know she had a son," Ramona said. "When did Helena St. Pierre find the time to have children? Who knew she had a son? Who knew she had sex? I thought the woman was a saint."

I nodded dumbly. Marina stood by the oyster bar and pretended to gag.

"Well," the assistant said, "don't you think the resemblance is amazing?"

"Who are his friends?" Ramona nodded at Dad's houseguests.

The assistant shook her head.

"I don't have any information about them."

Ramona sat with one leg up against the canvas chair's arm. In her lap was her videocamera. She raised the chunky machine onto her shoulder and pointed her microphone at me.

"You must have felt horrible the last few days. Tell French Canada how you are feeling."

"Well, you know"—pausing, as I made my first public statement—"someone died. My mother is dead." It came out sounding as though I were a zombie.

"Yes, right. How did you find out? How did you receive the information?"

Her eyes were set wide and her mouth fell open, revealing comely white teeth and pink gums. She had a flirty look, a haze of arousal fogging her eyes, I thought. My stomach dropped as I came upon a dirty realization of my own.

The dressing room door cracked open. Richard waved me in.

I excused myself from Ramona. Marina was watching me, frowning in a way that made her look less pretty. I moved past the musicians and roadies and managers and disc jockeys and into the Urethra Franklin dressing room, all leather couches and leafy plants and baskets of fruit. There was bottled water chilling in a huge ice bucket. The members of the band broke out in applause when they saw me, as if I were the one who had just given a concert. Richard, his right eye puffy and purple, clamped a hand on my shoulder and was set to introduce me to the band individually, when I asked him how much he had paid my father for Helena St. Pierre's address.

SUNDAY

The big blowup came that afternoon in the living room. I found him in his recliner, already dressed for the viewing. He was in a dark blue suit, the top button of his pressed shirt undone, a sleepy look on his face. His legs were crossed and in his open hand he held his tie, neatly folded, red with white stripes.

My father saw me and yawned.

"I wasn't expecting you."

I apologized out of reflex.

"There's no reason to say you're sorry. I was expecting someone else. And Marina—she's the one you're looking for, right—she's out this moment with Louise. I asked them both to go out for the day so I could be here by myself, at least until my guest arrives. I haven't had time to think."

I told him I needed to ask him something.

"Ask me anything," he said sweetly. "You're my son." My father had an arsenal of complicated expressions. Like this one—this sweet, gentle look on his face. He could blindside me with unexpected demonstrations of generosity and compassion. This was called charm.

"First, sit down," he said. "You're making me nervous."

It was in the air, I thought. Fatigue in the room like humidity. A jungle of exhaustion. Dad coughed into his fist and cleared his throat. I could tell he wasn't in the mood to listen, that his reedy voice, so whiny and ironical, was already craggy from talking. I sat on the far end of the couch, away from him.

"I don't know if they're going to be here much longer, Saul. I'm talking about my houseguests. Louise Gordon and Marina Finch. They're nice girls. They're smart girls. But they'll be gone sooner than you think. Women. They land where the wind blows. I'm saying this now for you to keep in mind in case you're becoming attached. I know, I know, you have something to say, though I feel obliged to speak my piece first. Age before beauty. I mean, they are beautiful young women, and it is nice to be appreciated, to be the object of appreciation, but I'm going to have to ask them to leave soon, because there's been too much excitement. It's fucking with my health. I can't shit properly. And if it's been many laughs having them around, it's been so with the knowledge that it isn't forever. Not that forever means anything. Cockroaches live forever. Your name on a marker and your piece-of-shit car and your kitchen and your cheapo hit single. We can't expect perfection to last more than seconds, minutes. You remember perfect moments like you sense the oven is on.

"I admit to being a poor father. But it's not been because I haven't cared about you. I tried and I tried. I got tired. It wasn't what I was suited for. But now you're eighteen years old, you can pretty much do as you please. You can hate me to your heart's fill, but you've turned out well, in any case. Perhaps in spite of me. Eighteen. I cared about you as much as I could. I got tired. Your mother had worn me out by the time you were born. You know how the saying goes: I'd rather go to jail than fall in love again. Set your clock by those words. I don't speak from lofty vistas, from blissful, snowcapped mountaintops, Saul, no, but from the gutter. She was the only person I have ever loved, fully and voluntarily. I tried to take her suffering and make it my own. I tried to see the world through her eyes. I did my utmost to give her what she wanted, but what she said she wanted didn't please her. We argued, we yelled and slept around on one another, we drank and did coke and pills, we spent entire weeks apart and got people who worked for us to relay hurtful messages. One night she said she wanted to leave me. I said she couldn't, I forbade it, and I sent her to the doctors in Montreal. The doctors talked to her and their diagnosis was that she wanted to leave me. All right, fine. I realized I couldn't keep her. So I told her to go. I told her she shouldn't feel obliged to stay. But then she decided, after stalling for a month, sleeping in another room, even packing her bags, that she didn't want to go anymore. She wanted a child instead, something she'd wanted but gave up on. Of all decisions to make. I went along with her to make her happy. You don't tell a woman what she wants, even if you might know better. If you're smart, you agree, you roll your eyes, then at night you kick the blankets from her feet.

"So she got pregnant after us trying for a year. She adored you. It made me jealous how she doted on you. I said we needed to tour again, and she thought it was a good idea, but when we did, it put her in a black mood, the blackest. She said she hated me. I told her again to go, and again she begged me not to let her. She couldn't keep her answers straight. I was tired, I had no heart. Not to say I wasn't surprised when she actually ran off, that she actually did. I'm sorry, Saulie."

"When did you get her address?"

He tilted his head a little and raised his eyebrows. The warmth on his face disappeared, some gear inside him turned, even as that smile struggled afloat on his face. He continued in the same level tone.

"Richard told you that, did he? That's your question?" He laughed. "*Saul*"—he looked at me incredulously—"I could always get her address if I'd wanted to. If you had bothered to ask me, I would have given it to you—for free. If you weren't so lazy, so self-absorbed. You should already know that. Don't waste my time. Don't be so fucking stupid. People asked me where she was and I said I didn't know. I was being honest, but they assumed that I couldn't find her—I only had to make a phone call. She would get mail, checks, for a few years after the fact, after her so-called mysterious disappearance. I mailed those to her grandmother—you never met her. She didn't want to see you. I sent the divorce papers to the old woman. Her grandmother, your great-grandmother, received them until she died a few years ago, then those two idiot cousins—you may have seen them on TV, Ricky and Ezra, those morons with their quiches and roadblocks, complaining about how bad they have it, when they lived quite nicely off Helena. Put Fatty through culinary college. Leni didn't want a penny, and they took advantage of her. Ricky and Ezra. They wanted to speak tonight at the viewing. I let them know the many ways they could fuck off.

"I had known she was in Bangkok for years. Before she died, her grandmother wrote me saying Helena was in Asia and that it was my marital obligation to make things right. It wasn't until maybe a year ago that I heard from her. Helena called me, asking about you. In case you're wondering, she wanted to know how you were. She asked to speak to you. When I told her I wouldn't allow it, she said that it was all right, she said she had forgiven me, prayed that I had turned to righteousness. She called in the middle of the night. Jana asked me who it was. I wouldn't say and we argued about that because she's always been a jealous woman. Then I hit her. That was the night your stepmother decided to leave me. In case you're keeping track of the score."

Dad yawned again, his mouth closing on a small burp. "I never sent her any mail. And so I thought that was that. Then about a month ago, she wrote me. She'd heard her own voice on the radio. Someone had recognized her. She asked me what I could do. Can you believe it? There was nothing to be done. She was furious. 'I won't have it,' she said. As belligerent as always. 'I won't have it.' She accused me of profiting on her pain. I did no such thing, but it gave me the idea. The return address was written on the envelope. I admit it—one reason I let Richard on her was to see what had become of her. I wanted to hear what she had to say. Maybe after all these years I had become curious. I've had people looking at me sideways, thinking nasty thoughts about me, surmising. Oh, hell, I thought. Richard wanted to hear my version of the story—at least I thought he did. It turns out he's no good, either. There were so many people sniffing around for an interview, who wanted to find Helena, and sooner or later they would have found her, with or without my assistance. I figured I may as well get a paycheque out of it."

"Where is it?"

"I put it in the bank."

"The letter she sent you?"

"No, the cheque."

"What about the letter?"

Dad groaned, out of impatience. "I threw it in the trash, Saul. Just like the note Felix brought with him, the one they found in her flat. I burned that without even opening it. Oh, don't look at me like that. *Don't.* Not in my house. It was addressed to me and I saw fit to burn it."

My father sighed. He closed his eyes for a moment, before they fluttered back open. He stood up and turned his back to me, he buttoned his top button, he ran the red-striped tie along the back of his neck, he slipped the tie underneath his starched white collar, he knotted his tie, then fastened it, wiggling his ass. Then he sat down, in his suit, looking toward the floor, a fan on the coffee table whipping back his hair.

I got up and started out of the room. I stopped at the kitchen entrance.

"You're a liar."

"Well, yes, Saulie, I am an inveterate liar," he said, his voice singsong and mocking. "What have I said that sounds untrue? You tell me."

"You never let her go," I said.

"Of course, she left on her own."

"You were too weak to keep her."

"Oh, right. Now I remember. I was too weak."

"She ran off with another man."

"Yes, she did. An old friend of hers. The guy with the book. The book everyone's talking about." Then he added, "Strange how Leni's death buoys us all up."

"She never loved you."

Dad nodded.

"You're right, that's very possible. She didn't." He picked a piece of lint from his slacks, held it up to his face, then watched it fall to the floor. "Is that all? I'm expecting company."

"She despised you. She thought you were vile and despicable. She left without warning, because if you knew she was leaving, you would've asked her to take me along."

"Don't be melodramatic. *Please.*"

"But she left without me. You couldn't control her. Your career depended on her voice, her stage presence, otherwise you'd still be working at the Salisbury House in Winnipeg. You thought you were doing it for her, but she didn't care about the music or the money, the things you got your kicks from. She loathed it. You did everything you could to keep her. You put her on anti-depressants, you told her she had contractual obligations to fulfill, you got her pregnant. You thought this was devotion, yet she loved someone else, and it made you bitter, it turned you angry and cheap."

We heard the doorbell ring, but Dad didn't move out of his seat. He let me finish, if not to humor me then because he was afraid. By now I was trembling, my voice cracking. I sounded stu-pid, like a TV detective, like a lawyer giving his final argument: I know, I know. But this was what I said: "It made you vengeful. And then you had your opportunity."

We heard the door unlock.

"Are you finished?" my father said. "Am I free to go?"

"You're responsible for her death."

Jana appeared at the other end of the kitchen.

"Saul," she said. "I wasn't expecting you here."

"That's what Dad said."

"Your father wanted to show me the kitchen."

She stared at the hole in the ceiling, then opened and closed the newly installed cabinets.

Dad brushed by me at the kitchen doorway.

Jana glared at him.

"What were you yelling about?"

"The same old. Saul was only putting me in my place. Giving me a regular tongue-lashing. I think I've been grounded. I can't leave the house for two weeks. My car privileges have been suspended."

"There you go again. This is a tough time for him. He needs your guidance. He's curious about his past. But what do you do? You joke. You make light of his pain. You stick your thing into little tarts. This is no way for a man your age to act."

"We were talking about the boy's mother. I suppose you were the one who filled his head with this nonsense."

"What nonsense?"

"That I was responsible for all this business," he said. "Look at him—he wants to hit his own father."

"I was telling him," I said to Jana, "what you told me."

Dad glared at me, his eyes dark and extra-squinty, disgust crawling across his face, a pitch-black scowl.

"And what did Jana tell you?" he asked. "What does Jana know about what happened?" He blinked. "Not a thing. Which means you know considerably less than nothing. I suppose it's easier to blame me. It was the same with your mother, and I imagine her hysteria passed into your blood. That's one thing you got from her."

Jana turned to me, her arms crossed. She thought it was time for me to leave.

The phone was ringing when I got home.

"Don't ask me how I got your phone number," said a man on the line. "I asked a couple of people—a friend of mine is an ex-detective. I had a brainstorm. I was watching the news, when I thought, Where is her son? Because no one asks what the kids think. But aren't they the ones with stories to tell? Aren't all our best stories the ones we pick up from our parents as children in our formative years, little creepy stories we half remember?"

"Who are you?"

His name was Leslie Erickson. "I was scanning through your parents' biography, the one I wrote way back when. I looked at it and saw your picture, you on a sled, age three, and I wondered, He must be of adult age right now. Knowing what I know about your parents' lives, there was so much I had to leave out. I bet you had an interesting childhood. Listen: How well do you do in your English classes? I mean, do you know a run-on sentence, split infinitives? Do you keep a diary? Were you ever abused? We can use that. You can tell me. Things you might think are perfectly harmless can seem hideously inhuman to others. Of course I can offer my services, over thirty years' experience in writing and editing, and then we can put it down, and you have your story— staring you in the face. If you want to appear in a national magazine, here it is. Don't worry if you think you're too unattractive for TV. There are plenty of heifers on screen. Let me give you my number. I mean, this is an opportunity. It's a story. The world needs stories. Let me ask you: How would you like to leave your mark on the earth?"

I said I'd think about it.

"Have you been talking to anyone else? *Fuck me.* Who is it?"

I went upstairs. There were shoes, polished, at the foot of my bed. My suit was laid out for me, slacks first, a coiled belt sitting on the fly, an ironed shirt placed over my jacket, both on hangers, the sleeves flung out, ready to embrace. A blue tie was slung around the jacket hanger.

I folded the clothes neatly on the back of a chair. I usually got eight hours of sleep a night, ten on weekends, back when I was moderately normal, I thought, as I stripped to my underwear and lay down.

I tried not to think about Helena St. Pierre. I tried not to think of squandered opportunities. Because maybe my father would have told me about her, her whereabouts, if only I had asked. That would be like my father, not to volunteer information, not for free, anyway. But I also figured that I had never really considered looking for my mother, that I was perhaps too lazy and unimaginative to seek her out, and that perhaps I secretly wanted her life to remain a secret. I had too much respect for mysteries. I was terrified of them.

I needed sleep. I would nap for a good hour, I decided. I would clear my head and think of pleasant things. I would dream about swimming in North Ontario with my grandparents; I would dream my favorite movies; I would dream about the great meals in my life, like the time I had really good Mexican or the very excellent Polish sausage of two weeks back. I would dream about sex the way I did before I started having it, without responsibility, without foreplay, without smells and spills and sounds.

Instead, I lay in bed thinking about my book deal.

My autobiography would be something. It would be sad and tawdry, so brief it could be printed on a Bazooka bubble-gum wrapper for fifth-graders, who would also buy my forthcoming collaboration with Urethra Franklin. There would be a comic-book version of my memoir, and a TV movie, which I'd insist on starring in. I'd play me, and some guy with wavy hair would be my old man, and we'd get that woman from the bikini-wax infomercial to be my dear departed mother. I would move to Hollywood, never to see anyone in this crummy town ever again, which was what I had wanted all along.

Of course, the book would have to come first. I could see myself on the jacket, a dumb frown on my face. It would be called *Child of Tragedy* or *Tears in Heaven: The Saul St. Pierre Story* or simply *Thanks, Dad.* I would get a ghostwriter, someone literary, but it would be only me autographing copies at supermarkets and book fairs. I would appear on those television shows where they took callers. It would be one of those shows with a five-second broadcast delay, where the host would tell the caller to turn down his set because of the Matterhorn-type echo of selfsame delay, which they'd have in order to cut off callers who turned out to be foulmouthed or racist or crazy, so that the viewers at home wouldn't hear a single offensive word. Some caller would be swearing at me, but they'd only see their host saying something like, "I guess he hung up," and me smiling like a bemused, mentally retarded mannequin.

The phone began to ring.

Navi was on the line: "Where have you been? You missed all the excitement."

"When?"

"On Friday, when we occupied the principal's office. It was great. I wish you had been there. They had to call in policemen in riot gear. We were all carried out, lame-duck style. They put handcuffs on me and took down all our names and asked us never to set foot on school property. Some guy spit on a cop and was put in a holding cell. We had coverage on three different stations in the Lower Mainland and a spot on CBC *Newsworld*—after the quiche thing had broken up. I think we really made a point."

"About what?"

"Exactly."

I told Navi how I had met Urethra Franklin the night before.

"They want to put my voice on record. The proceeds would go to collective presses in Montreal and The Hague. I haven't decided whether I'll do it. I don't know. What do you think of their music?"

"My sisters like it a lot."

"Well, they're huge with eighth-graders."

"The drummer's kind of cute."

"I met her, too. Her name's Dorit. She's sort of bloated in real life."

"I like round girls."

I checked the clock radio on my night table. I needed to be at the funeral home in an hour. I sat up in my bed and began to get dressed.

"Have you talked to Rose lately?" I asked Navi. I had the phone wedged between my ear and my shoulder as I slid my pants on.

"Why don't you just call her?"

"Not likely. We have a viewing for the body tonight."

"I know. I saw it on the news."

"I'm pretty good, actually."

"I've been worried about you."

"I'm pretty good."

I was feeling lighthearted, oddly enough. Almost giddy. It was almost over. They'd have put her body in the ground by tomorrow afternoon, and then everyone would leave, Richard and Andreas, Louise and Marina, and practically everything would be as it was before. I would get to sleep and maybe Rose would return my calls. I would attend classes so I might have a chance of passing my exams. All this business would calm down.

I put on my jacket. There was a full-length mirror on my door, so I inspected myself. My tie was crooked and I needed gel in my hair, but otherwise I was looking pretty sharp. I appeared somber and sincere, maybe a little too serious. I made a goofy face. I flipped my eyelids inside out and smiled with all my teeth and gums. I started throwing punches, jabs in front of the mirror.

"I bet you didn't know I've been offered a book deal for my life story."

"Cool," Navi said. "I've been writing mine since I was eleven."

This was probably true. On a wall in Navi's room, next to his framed honor roll certificates, was a picture of Subcomandante Marcos, leader of the Zapatista movement in Chiapas, Mexico, that he'd gotten off the Internet—two eyes staring forth from a ski mask. Subcomandante Marcos was Navi's idol. For an English composition assignment the year before he had written a surprisingly humorless short story about how he was actually Marcos's only son, conceived while the Samra family was on vacation in Oaxaca in 1980. In the story, Marcos—disguised as a friendly Jesuit priest and tour guide—kidnapped Mrs. Samra. He placed his finger over the lips of Navi's mother, and they disappeared into the hills outside town for "reeducation." What followed was rather indecent, considering that the woman in the story was supposedly his mother.

I was waiting by the door when Jana got home. "Give me five minutes," she said. And she kept her word, much to my surprise. She came bounding down the stairs in a hat and a dark dress with white buttons running down the middle, a sun-bleached expression on her face. We were both in a bright mood, it seemed.

We climbed into the car. The seats were warm, the air inside felt like melted rubber, and I was getting hot in my suit. I rolled down the window and wished for air-conditioning. We started out of the parking lot.

"It's the kitchen I wanted."

On Trunk Road we pulled over to let a fire truck pass.

"Your father wants you to move back in with him."

"I won't," I said.

"He thinks it might be better."

"What about you, then?"

"He thinks I should move back, too."

"You can't," I said. "You two are divorced."

"*Saul.*"

"Christ, why does everybody say that? Do people have trouble with my name?"

The fire truck was out of view now. Jana pulled back into traffic.

"I thought you were marrying Dale," I said. "All of a sudden, he's out of the picture. Have you thought about him at all?"

"Yes," Jana snapped back. Her left-turn blinker was still on, making its clicking sound. There was something wrong with the blinker, and it didn't automatically turn off. It clicked like a panting dog.

"Your blinker's on."

"Oh." She turned it off. "Of course I've thought about Dale. I think about Dale. I've given thought. And it's not as though I've come to any decision yet. For either of them. I never gave Dale an answer, and I haven't given your father one, either. But it's not that simple." She paused. "Ian's different."

"What do you mean by that?"

"It means that, for him, I'm willing to do things I'll regret later."

"Sounds kind of lousy."

"It is."

"Do you want my advice, Jana?"

She smiled, then nodded patronizingly.

"Don't act rashly."

Jana laughed. We both laughed.

"Okay," she said.

Jana liked to tell the story about how I ran into her arms the very first time I saw her, when I came to live with her and Dad. We were at the airport, my grandmother was holding me by my collar—that was how my father was raised, and it explained a lot. She was saying how shy a four-year-old I was, but before she could even give her warning, I had pried myself away from her dry, bony hand. It was 1984, three and a half years after the St. Pierres ended. Jana wasn't sure whether she would be a good mother, a good mother figure, to a boy too swift and willful for Ian's arthritic parents. She was twenty-one, and the youngest child in her family—her two sisters had already moved out of the house before she was even in grade school. She was not used to being married quite yet, not used to calling herself a wife.

And I came to her, she said, in tiny denim overalls, a half-Indian boy with watery eyes and a bowl cut, full of misplaced love. I placed my hands on her round cheeks.

As she told it, I kissed her square on the lips, and her heart melted.

We stopped at an intersection right before the funeral home. I could hear a lawn mower buzzing in the distance, out of view. "You're looking good today." She watched me, this dreamy glaze over her eyes. "Helena would be proud to have such a beautiful son. It would make her feel better about herself." The car started moving. "She was a vain woman, Saul. She was deeply infatuated with herself. You'd figure if you spent your life obsessed with yourself, you'd pick up an insight or two. Well, not the case. You should know that. Don't look for explanations. She was plain dumb, is all."

"Stupid people should know better."

"They should."

I raised my fist in the air and shook it. "Stupid people, when will you learn?"

We entered the chapel from the rear, to the row reserved for the immediately bereaved, where my father sat alone, the pew that allowed an unobstructed view of the open coffin and the floral arrangements encircling it like some Druid monument. Middle-aged heads turned, as if by cue, from practice and teamwork and cunning, when we approached. Neither of my parents had much family left, none who showed up. The mourners here were friends of my parents, musicians from Yorkville: family friends from out of town whom I'd met on a few occasions, all nice folks who played music at one time or another, a little loopy from too much prescription medication for joint inflammations and antisocial tendencies, who suffered from deafness in one ear and ringing sensations in the other. They were men in deerskin vests and bolo ties, wearing graying lambchops, wiry guys with high foreheads and veiny forearms, session players who followed their own style, all skinny leather ties and short-sleeved cotton shirts and scraggly facial hair, single earrings and sweatbands onstage, a dress code for rockers in midlife as rigid as a street gang's. They brought their wives, floppy-breasted women carrying big handbags. The room was full. They'd been waiting for this; they'd taken days off and driven eighteen hours straight or caught standby flights.

There was a volume swell at our entrance, my entrance. I was recognized, their eyes locking onto me as they tried to locate that resemblance, the love-child aura that followed me like the smell of a ripe egg. They mumbled about me over the sound of the organist playing in a corner, blocked from view by a halo of carnations. This lasted precisely one moment, hardly two bars of the organist's tune. Soon enough, the eyes of the room resettled on my mother's body, lying in a sleek silver coffin with black panels and brass handles along its sides, next to the lectern in front of us. She was the centerpiece, a figurine, a drowsy debutante, her lips and cheeks rouged, her hair swept back, in her farewell performance.

Dad was talking to Father Felix, who stood crouched over him and with his long body cast a shadow across him. Dad peered up at him. Father Felix moved back to the lectern and began shuffling papers. Jana sat between me and Dad. She leaned over and whispered something into his ear. He smiled.

There was a box of tissues next to me on the pew.

I could hear sniffling, mixed with the general mumble of the crowd. Programs folded and unfolded, asses slid down pews, investments were divulged softly.

I turned around and looked for people I knew. I searched until I found Marina and Richard, four rows back. They waved at me. Marina was wearing a black sleeveless number, her hair in pigtails, her arms creamy white.

I started to stand up for a better view of the body.

Jana looped a hand around my elbow and pulled me back into my seat.

Father Felix cleared his throat into the mike.

"In the name of the Father, the Son, and the Holy Spirit."

We said the Lord's Prayer. I mouthed along from memory, though I didn't know where I'd had the chance to learn it. We weren't a religious family, not even my grandparents, who were nominally Catholic and went to Mass regularly out of respect for their parents' memory. I thought of belief in God as a demonstration of a child's love for his mother and father. I didn't think about Him, not usually, only when I was frightened, because I figured hell was a reasonable concept. We had jails in real life. We had punishment. We tortured.

When weren't hymns ugly business, when weren't they saccharine, up-tempo numbers? They were entirely unconvincing. Jana held her program up beside me so we could both sing from the lyrics printed there, but I felt compelled to keep my mouth closed, my eyes on the coffin. My mother had been in the choir in Thailand. I imagined her singing these words. She must have really lost her marbles. Either it was a chemical imbalance or some tricky recessive gene, maybe even the Holy Spirit itself taking residence in her heart. But to end up singing this by her own free will—she might as well have stayed with my father.

Heaven had no local equivalent.

Dad was holding up well. He was practically barking out the words to the hymns, just as he did the Our Father. He sneaked glances at the coffin and dug his hands in his pockets, his shoulders hunched inward, his chin dropping to his chest.

The hymns went by slowly. I rocked back and forth on my feet.

There was Dad, Jana, and I, together. There was Dad and my mother reunited. There was my mother and I, together at last, before the chapel audience. It was like a cruel TV show, something Richard might have hosted back in Germany, where secret guests lurked backstage in soundproof rooms and curtains drew open to reveal kitchen appliances. In that case, my mother was a dummy prize, a parting gift. A small brown face, a young woman's face, her cheeks hollow and her tiny nose rounding up on a blunt point, and her hair glossy black, her neck long and thin and framed by the frilly collar of the white summer dress she was to be buried in. I wanted to touch her. I wondered whether I would have the nerve to touch the body. I allowed myself to think dark thoughts.

Gord spoke first, reading from a piece of creased loose-leaf.

"I see a lot of familiar faces in the audience, and it's nice to see everyone again after all these years, even under these circumstances. Everyone here is looking prosperous. And much wiser." A few in the audience chuckled. Gord smiled briefly. "When Ian asked me to say something about her, I was left scratching my head about what to talk about. I really didn't know her too well for someone who played in her band for six years, not as well as I would have liked. She was quiet and let Ian speak for her, she let the music speak for her. But I know she was a kind woman who treated everyone on the road or in the studio with respect. She wasn't stuck-up at all for such a big star, and we all know a lot of stuck-up musicians." More laughter. "She cared about people. I remember her being a good mother who was very proud of her son when he was born. From what I hear, she was a religious woman, and she treated the poor with the same sort of, um, compassion that I saw in her all those years ago. In fact, my wife Nadine and I have decided to name our first child after Helena." Gord broke into a smile; some people chuckled again. He nodded, then stepped away from the lectern, red-faced, people congratulating him when he sat down.

The speakers who followed him didn't say much that was different. There were more people from the band, a few who knew my mother back in the Yorkville days. Their memories were fuzzy. They talked about Helena St. Pierre the libertine, the artist, the singer with a social conscience, but this was old news. I had heard it all before. I felt jilted.

It was my father's turn to speak. He ambled up, took a quick peek at the body, and then settled at the lectern, his hands gripping its sides.

I stood to leave.

"Saul, sit down," Jana said, her face severe, a little impatient.

"I'm sorry."

My father watched me go without saying a word. I moved down the aisle and out of the chapel, keeping my eyes to the ground.

Mr. Dirk, the funeral guy, in the same dark suit, stood in the reception area with a couple of young female assistants, who were busy arranging a large metal coffee dispenser and trays of biscuits on tables.

He looked up at me.

"Sir, is there a problem?"

I shook my head.

"Refreshments will be ready in ten minutes."

I nodded.

He turned away, and as though she had been hiding behind him, Louise appeared, weeping in a corner of the room. She was wearing a man's dark short-sleeved shirt. Her lips were shiny from gloss. She held in her hands a ball of crumpled beige tissue.

"I thought he was brilliant," she was saying between sobs.

"I'm sorry." I held out my hand, and placed it on her elbow. This was what Jana usually did, before she drew someone into an embrace.

"I know why you're upset with him," she said. "I know why."

"It's okay." I pulled her toward me. She leaned against my bony chest and quaked.

"He wanted Helena to come out of hiding. A real live TV reunion. Asshole." She dabbed the tissue against her eyes. We could hear my father's whiny, excitable voice inside the chapel, pleading his case, memorializing a woman he loathed. "I'm so stupid. I'm so—I'm so disappointed."

I nodded. I knew how she felt. I really did. I knew what it was like to admire Ian St. Pierre. There was a time when I wanted to walk like him, to grow out my hair like him, to have the same sweaty callused fingers. I loved him to pieces. I loved my father for his best qualities: his wit, his determination, his laughter, even his occasional kindnesses. When he was at his best, I wanted him to be like that all the time. And it killed me that I wasn't good enough, not worth the trouble, for him to feel the same about me. It slayed me. My mother was my first unrequited love, but my father was a close second. I knew exactly how Louise felt.

A lawn mower rolled out of the parking lot from a shed next to the mausoleum. The lawn mower was green with yellow trim and yellow hubcaps. The driver was a man in a pair of overalls who wore safety goggles and big headphones. I sat outside the chapel, on a bench in the garden with ruffly purple flowers and a pond, watching the mower rumble down the paved roads that crisscrossed the cemetery. Beside me on the bench was a man in a dark sports jacket, a white shirt, and black tuxedo pants, glossy gray lines running down each pant leg. His hair was cautiously combed forward, and tinted wire-rims fell to the end of his nose. On his jacket was an "It Takes Two to High-Five" button. He sucked on a cigarette.

Nathan Shaw pushed his glasses up his nose with his pinky finger.

"Why aren't you inside?" I asked.

"I got chicken."

"You're my mother's old boyfriend."

He nodded.

"She left my dad for you."

He had a sick look on his face.

"No, she just left."

Even then he dressed as though he'd lost a bet. It wasn't the clothes that drew my mother to the man thirty years before. When they first met, he looked ridiculous in his paisley shirts, chasing the zeitgeist's slippery tail. By the time they were in Toronto, he was all clean-cut and geeky, like some Korean orphan brought back by missionaries, wearing Salvation Army handouts. He was a clumsy Chinese kid with a sharp mouth and a beautiful native girlfriend. She liked him because he was, in private, timid and sweet. He was twenty, two years older than she. She was his first. Intimacies aside, he kept his distance. He didn't drink like Ian would, and he wasn't as big an asshole, but he was sometimes arrogant and willful to the point of whininess—just like Ian. There was a wiriness to his body, a tenseness in his behavior which was arousing. When she tickled him on the couch, he would wrestle her down, and he seemed to take it a little too seriously. Sometimes she could picture him hitting her.

In Toronto, they lived in a room in Kensington, above a bakery. He worked at his uncle's restaurant, where he stole singles and change from the till, and sat on the toilet downstairs or on an upturned milk crate in the back alley, reading newspapers left over from the breakfast rush. It was only a matter of time until his uncle fired him, until the Chinese family goodwill expired, but he was hanging on to the easy work as long as he could.

Nathan taught Leni Sinclair what she knew about ambition. Namely, that she required some. "If you're going to get any-where," he said, half joking, "you'll need someone to run your life. And maybe lose five pounds." He had Hemingway as a cub reporter in mind when he decided to move to Toronto. At night, Mondays through Saturdays for an entire year, she watched him punch away at the vainglorious Olivetti, pull sheets out of the machine, and pencil in margin notes.

He sat near the edge of his wicker-backed chair, in slippers, his thin ankles crossed, in search of the next word, wriggling like a blind black man in front of his piano.

It's just annoying, she thought, this so-called dedication. It was Protestant and uptight and self-denying and everything she wasn't about.

He hated the books she read: Kerouac, Hesse, the Brautigan pocket editions, *Selected Quotations of Chairman Mao.* The plays of Joe Orton. They never saw the end of most of the movies they went to, because he insisted on storming out halfway through. Antonioni and *Sansho the Bailiff* and Godard, that Swiss cunt who liked beginnings, middles, and ends, though not necessarily in that order.

Leni liked everything she saw; she was an enthusiast, an avid participant, before her meltdown years later. She liked to wear a green Yugoslavian embroidered blouse, back when Yugoslavian fashion had a looser grip on the public imagination. She had gotten the blouse from a friend who said she'd stolen it from the costume closet of the Chatham Little Theatre.

She volunteered at a co-op gallery next to a coffeehouse.

Art wasn't supposed to be drudgery. It was play. You lived art; you lived your life as art. It was detergent advertising copy, and *Blondie* with the bubbles whited out and filled in with British cuss words and sound collage and party-chat transcripts, and recontextualized underwear hung on lines with orange plastic pegs.

He wouldn't even let her read his book.

She began to leave the house without him.

Somebody at the gallery needed help with his boat, so a group of them went over to paint its underside one weekend.

Another person brought a guitar. Leni impressed her fellow boat painters by singing "Greensleeves," then "Sugar Mountain" and "Norwegian Wood."

He was not pleased about her nude modeling, and was livid when she did it in public. Because she asked him to, he went to her Happening, to see her spread out on the divan, airing her naughty bits on a downtown street and almost threw punches at some hooting men, almost hit Ian St. Pierre. He paid off her fine with his stolen tips.

He thought she wasn't contributing enough to the household economy.

She thought the book was secretly about her.

She wanted to be an artist.

She wanted to reinvent it—the world.

She wanted to sing.

He thought she was loose.

One afternoon, the Greek landlady is on her knees planting mousetraps in the hall. "Your husband is out looking for you," the old woman says, without bothering to look up. "Or maybe he say he is going to Chinese restaurant. I don't know. Don't bother me. I am busy woman."

Leni unlocks the door and finds herself alone in their messy room with his manuscript lying around.

She's shocked by how little he knows about her, how she's portrayed, alternately, as shrew and fool.

She is halfway through when he comes in.

She throws the telephone at him.

To start, he says, it's not about you.

It's like a diary.

Secondly, you're not supposed to be reading this. This is private.

Then you admit—it is a diary.

You're invading my privacy.

She wags a finger like some Prohibitionist marm, a figure of moral sobriety: You invaded mine first.

She starts throwing her underwear in a knapsack.

You're a shithead. My grandmother was right about you.

Thirdly, you're only upset because it's honest.

She says she hates him, she says she's about to leave, a threat she's made before, one he doesn't take seriously since he's long stopped taking what she says seriously. Ian and Nathan would agree: She likes arguments and tantrums; her face tingles in a nice way when she wails. She gets lost. She barely finds her way back home after she leaves. She just avoids getting on a bus to Etobicoke, wherever that is, that's how helpless and hopeless she is.

She hasn't said one word whether the book was any good.

Slut, he says. The space between them has been pregnant with that word.

Would it kill her to say one nice thing about the book?

You're a slut, he says. Go off and sleep around. Fuck everyone in the city.

He sits down and starts tapping away again at the typewriter, maybe because she hates its sound.

Whore.

The room smells like patchouli and a gerbil farm. There is an unfinished papier-mâché sculpture of a yak on a table. There is a dying fern next to it. There is a mason jar half filled with apple cider next to that. The light is depressing. Nathan said he hated being in direct sunlight. He's funny about a lot of things. She throws the typewriter off the table. It crashes against a chair, then smacks the ground with a metallic thud and ring. He grabs her by the arms, afraid for his stuff.

"You're going to hit me, aren't you?" she asks.

"No."

"Yes, you are."

It's as though she dares him, as though she doesn't think he's got it in him. It's a test, and he has no choice but to follow through. He throws her to the ground—it's easier than he has thought it would be, and he's thought about it more than once— then lands his foot between a couple of ribs. It almost sounds like laughter when she screams. He hasn't even hurt her. He wants to kick her again, but then she really starts to wail, a scream like an angry teakettle, like a startled cat, her hands in front of her face. She rolls away, flings herself against the arm of their upholstered loveseat.

The guy who owns the boat—Ned the painter—has already offered to put her up. She's been thinking this over. She takes her clothes, she takes her battered body and leaves.

Helena. Nathan listens to the radio and buys a couple of their records, listens to them on the armchair swirling the Cardhu in its tumbler, lingers over magazine photos, a *Rolling Stone* interview, described in another catatonic *Maclean's* spread, rereads the articles about her hospital stays for exhaustion, a piece about her having brunch with Abbie Hoffman in Montreal in 1976, but he doesn't think too much about her. Well, maybe a little. Once, in 1973 or '74, he watches Trudeau in a buckskin jacket on TV with his hippie wife and furrows his brow. There's something defiant in his vanity, a fussiness that softens his laser-guided political heart. Here he is, on television, blending in at a St. Pierres show in

Ottawa. The first prime minister who can get mellow. His wife, Margaret, is some magical gift to his vanity.

In his bathrobe at one in the afternoon, he sorts through the mail, thinking, sarcastically, this is easy, this is the life, at the joy of daylight squandered. He picks up the newspaper.

But then he reads about the birth of her son, and he gets depressed. Saul St. Pierre, a New Year's child, 1980. The woman he knew wouldn't have had a child. What is wrong with her?

She looks less human every time a photo of her is published. She's gotten so thin. There's nothing in her eyes.

He decides to write to her. To the effect of: Congratulations, remember me, I was thinking about you, anyway hope you're well, I'm doing fine, I remember that time, do you, maybe sometime, if you feel like it, we should get together, well, anyway, take care. He is too nervous to write anything very personal. He's surprised when she responds. They exchange notes. Then she calls him while she's on tour, confides, confesses her unhappiness, her difficulties, people whispering about its being postpartum depression, but she's *positive* that isn't the case. They talk about child-rearing. They agree that the approach in that book, that says you leave the kids wailing alone in their rooms all night, is too terrible to imagine. He hangs up when his wife—the gentle woman who accepts his fear of the free enterprise system and pays the rent— awakens. It feels good, oddly good, invigorating. He feels guilty preemptively.

She suggests they meet at the Labor Day show. She's been planning her departure, hasn't told anyone about it. Go to Vancouver. There'll be a ticket for him at the entrance. After the show, he can give the road manager his name and she'll meet him. They can be alone and have coffee or something.

You need to come get me, she tells him.

"I need someone to write my memoirs," I said.

"So soon?" he asked.

"It's now or never, really."

"You could put pen to paper yourself," Nathan said. He stubbed his cigarette butt against the heel of his shoe. "They say it's therapeutic."

"Or you could do it for me."

"That's just laziness."

"Maybe."

"I don't even know you."

"Use your imagination," I said.

He smiled and shook his head.

"Now who's being lazy?"

He's on the floor, though he decides to stay away from the swell of flesh pressing against the stage. How long has it been since his last concert? It must be years.

He doesn't like the smell of sweat, the stray elbows, the wolf whistles.

The roadies have finished setting up the stage, which remains empty a few minutes longer.

The crowd applauds.

She appears, in a white skirt and a billowy white blouse with puffy sleeves, and dark cowboy boots. Her husband steps onstage wearing sunglasses. His hair comes down to his shoulders. They both look thin, worn haggard from travel. She doesn't have that glow, that motherly glow—almost unreal, almost concocted, like a trial experiment from a research lab at Johnson & Johnson. The husband takes his place in the back with the band, leaving her out front. She seems to acknowledge the crowd with a shy smile fluttering on her mouth.

He's here only on a lark; he's lied to his family and made the four-hour flight only to say hello. He's made no promises.

He moves into the crowd.

He wants to see the whites of her eyes.

She's two inches tall from where he's standing. They've made her prettier, put magenta eye shadow and lipstick on her, sprayed and molded her hair, bleached her teeth—which had already been capped. She's like a human jukebox, standing in front of the microphone, mouthing song after song. He's never heard her sing live before. It's a little husky and slightly off-key, something that takes people time to get used to. Her voice booms. It has a belly. It leaves a tread. He doesn't really know any of the songs. They're up-tempo country rock and lilting, buttery ballads that seem to melt into one another. She says very little to the audience, only polite thank yous and brief introductions to songs, but it comes off coquettish in her little-girl manner.

He's proceeding through the layers of people, most of whom move aside when he brushes against them. These are gentle folk. Some are dancing, all sway in one way or another. Some of the women hold their hands over their heads and dance in a self-consciously sexy way. He gets maybe fifteen feet from the stage, enough to see the spit from her mouth and her face beaten down by the stage lights—red, blue, purple. He's light-headed from the humidity.

He feels himself being swept up in awe. His spirit lifts from his body and settles on his shoulders for a better view. She looks good, entranced in the music and burrowing into herself, her eyes staring past the crowd. He tries to push farther in, but it's harder going. The people in front of him have linked arms or something. These are diehards, the ones who feed off this proximity. He can see the logic. She's like a movie star, not a bombshell, but the actress who steals your heart, the one who plays the soiled, repentant woman in movie adaptations of Russian novels, a star who inspires newfound domestic urges and your worst, most syrupy impulses, a perfectly soft-mouthed woman with a bar of moonlight across her face, whose on-screen tears cleave your heart.

She seems maybe to catch his face in the audience, or so he thinks. She looks down at the stage and finishes the tune.

Then she rushes offstage, her husband's eyes following her suspiciously. Nathan starts away, sees a pair of security men at a side entrance and goes toward them. But the crowd around him isn't moving, nor are the lights back on. People are waiting for an encore.

Ten, twenty minutes pass and she hasn't appeared. A "Bullshit" chant is started somewhere in the cheap seats. He remembers that documentary he saw about Altamont. Only a little while back he read about a woman who needed a fortune's worth of dental work when she was winged by a piece of guitar debris at a Who concert. He imagines little kids being pressed against a metal fence. He thinks like the parent he is, and a wave of nausea briefly overtakes him. Some provinces have already banned festival seating. The people here, though, seem like responsible citizenry. A good age range, a lot of young couples. Suddenly he feels awkward about being by himself. He usually thinks twice about going to films alone when his wife is too tired. He definitely doesn't go out alone on Fridays or holidays. The band returns to the stage without her. The audience throws pennies and nickels at them, and some people rush the stage. They move all at once to get by security. When Ian comes back onstage, hopes are raised, but then he walks off with a sour look on his face. People are mad. They push over the gates and step on people in front. A guard slams a fist into the gut of a man aiming for the drum set. Somebody jumps on the back of the guard, scratches his face.

There's a stampede in the other direction and more people trip over one another. Nathan stays calm, trying not to bump into anyone. He wonders what he'll say to her, where they'll go. He starts mouthing something for when they finally meet, when a security guard places a hand flat against his chest. Nathan gives his name. He's expected backstage, he explains. The guard speaks into a walkie-talkie, repeating his name. He waits for an answer, then shakes his head.

MONDAY

Marina called the morning of the funeral. I gave her directions to the house and waited for her at the park outside our complex. Kids were running around the jungle gym. Next to the swing set, a poodle rolled on the grass, its hind legs pedaling in the air. Marina approached from the opposite side of the park in a white tank top and khaki shorts. Her shoulders swayed and her heels scuffed the grass. There was something rubbery about her walk that I liked. It made her look young, or my age.

"We had breakfast with your dad. Good old Ian. He gave us our walking papers, then he dumped the waffles on our plates. He wants us out by Wednesday. I wasn't surprised. Do you know what I'm saying? I've been getting that vibe. I'm happy to get going, in fact. Louise wants to leave soon—this afternoon, maybe. She's not taking it well. She thinks it's something she did. Don't look at me like that. Of course it was stupid. She spends a week here and goes crazy for an old man. She's your garden-variety crackpot— obviously. But why do guys have to be such utter and hopeless pricks? They pretend like they're letting you off gently because they think you just might be that stupid." She paused, then looked at me. "I wanted to see you in case I didn't get another chance."

"You're going?"

She nodded. "I guess you better make up with your girl-friend," she said. "What's her name again—Rose, right?" I told her it was. "Rose," she repeated, considering it, with a wan smile. She looked so perfectly breezy. I was unhappy to see her go, heart-broken possibly, but I wasn't going to say anything. By remaining silent I hoped to pass myself off as grown-up and sensible, but it was hard being, I hate to say it, brave. "I bet you won't even remember me in two weeks."

She waited for a response, then looked to the ground.

I led her home, into my unpresentable, squalid home. Not that I had many qualms about cleanliness, but I felt a twinge of shame as I kicked a pair of my underwear from the stairway landing.

Jana was reading in the living room when we came in. She put down her magazine, and her hands knotted into fists. I introduced her to Marina.

"I'm a friend of Ian's," she said.

"I know." Jana paused. "Saul told me." She smiled, her jaw locked, chained, and deadbolted. "Would you like some coffee? Or tea? I can make both."

"We're going upstairs, Jana," I said. She gave me a funny look, which I chose to ignore.

We took the twelve lime-green–carpeted steps up to my room. Marina stood by my desk and stared out my window toward the parking lot. My reading lamp was on.

"Are you writing something?" she asked.

"A letter." I lunged over to the desk, folded three sheets of loose-leaf, and put them in my pocket.

"Man of mystery. I like that."

"It's none of your business." My voice suddenly cracked. "Nothing you'd be interested in."

"I'll take your word."

Marina pointed to one of the matching silver frames Jana had put on my dresser. A school portrait. I wore a T-shirt and pin-striped overalls, in front of a blue backdrop.

"How old were you here?"

"I think I was eight."

"You look adorable."

"Thanks."

"And this one?"

"I was five, I think." I was standing in front of a canoe on a lake, an orange life jacket engulfing my face. Beside me, a silver-haired man held two fishing poles. "That's my grandfather." Even after my father took custody of me, I would visit my grandparents in the summers, until they died.

Marina smiled.

"He's a nice-looking guy."

"I miss him," I said. "He passed away when I was twelve." I thought of him now as I stared at a picture I normally paid little attention to. His stomach would bulge from a short-sleeved cotton shirt, and his pants were held up by thick red suspenders. He was a barber. I remembered jars of liquid colored blue like sinister potions, into which he'd dip his combs, and his customers, wiry gray men in plaid sweaters who stepped into the shop, the local paper tucked under their arms. Grandfather would hum "Lily of the Valley" as he lathered soap, before putting the straight-edge against their necks. His face was pink, with folds of loose skin that hung from his jaw. He had watery blue eyes. His fingers were stubby—like my dad's—his nails kept short and filed, gray hair on his knuckles. He wore two rings: a gold wedding band and a pinky ring with a blue stone.

His thick mustache was stained yellow from nicotine. I missed his mustache. He would let me play with it after dinner, once he'd had a couple of glasses of Irish whiskey. When I went off to bed, he would kiss me, and his mustache would feel scratchy and his breath would smell of alcohol. I used to stare at the bottle through the glass of the locked liquor cabinet. It was squat like a milk bottle with a stubby neck. The liquid inside was a faint yellow. And although I didn't read at the time, the label of the bottle read "Bushmills." The name my father immortalized in 1973.

"Where are you going?" I asked.

"Don't know. Louise thinks she wants to take a term off and keep traveling, though she might change her mind. Actually, it's not so hard getting around and meeting people. We thought Ian was going to be this recluse who lived off in the woods some-where, like a male version of Helena, drinking malt liquor and collecting child porn, but here he is in a suburb, accessible by pub-lic transit. Who knows? I guess we'll go wherever the buses take us. A Romanian dramaturge Louise wrote to finally replied, though we're not planning to go that far." She stopped and bit her thumb. "Can I ask you a question?"

I nodded.

"Are you going to forget about me?"

"I don't think so."

"You don't think so?"

"I mean, no."

"I don't believe you, not a word of it," she said. "You've got better things to do. I've accepted it. Otherwise, I'd ask you to run away with me. There's no hope for me. Don't deny it. I bet if I see you on the street ten years from now, you won't recognize me. I'll be on a corner busking for my dinner, and you won't even throw one thin dime into my violin case."

She said this sweetly and wistfully. And I figured she was right. She made a violin-bowing gesture with her hands again, just as she had at the doughnut shop, though this time she closed her eyes as if in rhapsody. Suddenly she seemed wise. If grace qualified as knowledge, then she was rich in wisdom. I closed my eyes, too, and tried to hear her invisible tune.

I borrowed Jana's car that morning because I was supposed to meet Richard at his motel, but first I wanted to drop off a letter to Rose. I drove to her part of town, where one cul-de-sac lined with BMWs and SUVs was followed by another. Crumpled and folded in my inside jacket pocket was the letter. It was written in red ballpoint and took up five single-spaced sides of loose-leaf, torn from a spiral notebook. In it, I asked Rose to forgive me because I didn't love her. I was hardly a prolific letter-writer, but now, when I had only this one thing to say, I was able to take up so much paper.

I had fooled her. I had pretended I felt deeply about her so I could sleep with her, like so many other boys I knew who joked about doing the same thing with their girlfriends. I never joked about it, and I supposed that was even worse, because I knew better—I knew what I did was cruel. Mean. Girls called boys "mean," as in "You're being so mean." Boys couldn't say "mean" without sounding like babies, without risking their claim to manhood. That was our only concern. Girls were the ones who had real worries. They had to actually keep from making babies.

About a block away I saw her, stepping out of the passenger-side front door of a car. She was in a trench coat, her hair in a ponytail. She looked pale and distracted, even sick. I figured she didn't want to see me. I wasn't looking forward to what she might say to me, or what her mother might say. She didn't notice me approaching in the car. She wobbled as she walked, as if she had a cramp. She stopped, put her hand to her forehead. Her mother helped her to the house, leading her by the elbow. Mrs. Clark looked back, but I was out of sight.

The motel room door had been left ajar. Richard's bed was unmade. Stuff lay fanned atop the television set, on display: a wallet, opened facedown, loose change and a passport, tobacco, rolling paper, and four purple Bic lighters. Andreas sat on Richard's bed, speaking German into the phone. Richard, in a white bathrobe and black leather slippers, sat in a chair changing channels on the TV, clicking the remote, which was bolted down to the night table. He nodded at me. The bruise on his face was now yellow.

"You are late," he said finally.

"I was busy."

"Andreas and I must leave soon."

I took Richard's cheque from my pocket and held it out for him to take.

"This belongs to you."

Richard waved it away.

"I can't take it."

"Tear it up, then. Flush it down the toilet," he said. "It is not important. It is not my money, anyway."

Andreas finished his phone conversation and hung up, then said something to Richard.

"It was good meeting you," Andreas said after a pause and a gulp. It was as though he'd swallowed the English language. "I wish you well."

He shook my hand, then stepped outside. Richard asked me to take a seat. I tried to refuse, but he insisted, so I sat across the room from him, in a chair next to a window and a brown air-conditioning unit.

"How do you do?" he asked.

"Fine."

"Fine? You left in a hurry yesterday at the chapel."

"I did."

"I understand. Both my grandmothers died last year. It is hard to see a corpse, yeah?"

I nodded.

"The flowers were shit," he said. "The music was shit. The priest was shit. The speakers were shit."

Richard faced the television, turning to me once and smiling glibly, flashing his gapped teeth, which seemed outlined in grime.

"Why are you so sad, Richard?"

"Because death is shit."

He crossed his bare legs and continued flipping channels. "Do you blame me for her death?"

"No."

"Thank you." Richard turned off the set. "The news is not what it used to be."

"When do you leave?" I asked.

"This evening we return to Germany. I leave abruptly, this is true. I have spoken to the network. We are no longer with them. They say I have devoted too much time and too much resources on this segment. The profit motive is a priority, of course. It is like this everywhere among the bourgeoisie, so is life. The network suggests I focus on the group Urethra Franklin. They say there are two nine-year-old boys, little fair-headed boys, who will claim one band member fondled them. The network would be interested in that. Already, they have become tired of Helena St. Pierre. They shall air what I have already recorded. This shall suffice, they tell me. Another producer is to edit the piece. I shall not allow them to have it. I have resigned. I shall burn the videotape before I surrender it to them. Maybe Andreas is burning it as we speak." He looked past me for a moment. "This is my promise to you, Saul. I am not a harlot. The piece is important to me. They will not fuck with my piece. They will not fuck with my video footage."

I crossed the room to the door.

I offered the cheque to him, held it as though to rip it up.

"Don't," Richard said, wincing. "Leave it here."

I held it out. He stood and took it, and put it in his pocket.

"You must keep in contact, Saul. I may need to speak to you in the future. You may wish to speak to me then."

"Sure."

"It is settled."

He sat down on the bed and rolled a cigarette, and asked me to toss him a lighter. I did.

He held the lighter in front of his face, the cigarette in his mouth. He put the lighter down.

"I shall quit."

What would my mother have thought of the throng gathered outside the church? The police had set up sawhorses to keep people from the path to the entrance, and they huddled against the barriers solemnly. They were mostly men well into middle age. Aside from sending hate mail and making death threats from untraceable mobile phones, people had left at my father's door flowers, wrapped in cream-colored paper or standing in jars half filled with water;

cards, some with sappy illustrated kittens, addressed to me; brown cardboard with pictures ripped out of magazines pasted on, with "Why?" written in marker underneath; and stuffed animals, mostly pocket-size white teddy bears. People couldn't get into the church itself, which was at full capacity, so they remained here on guard, as if this were another St. Pierres concert, snapping photographs and playing "Bushmills Threnody" on tape recorders, especially now, as former members of the St. Pierres' touring band and Father Felix stood ready to help carry my mother's coffin inside.

The car stopped behind the hearse, whose back door was already open. The coffin was wheeled to the steps of the church, then lifted by the pallbearers. What a gorgeous coffin, I thought, in spite of myself. The sun was warm against my face. I got out of the car first, followed by Jana and my father.

"This is a fucking nightmare," Dad muttered. Cameras snapped and flashed at him.

"Look at the turnout," Jana said. She almost squealed. "Do you think you'll have as many people at your funeral?"

Dad shot her a dirty look.

I wondered who wouldn't be curious about their own burial. When I was younger, I would imagine watching my funeral from heaven, seeing my father and Jana, my friends and classmates, teachers, in hats and white gloves, all of them clawing at the casket, weeping for me. And then I would see a strange woman emerge from the gaggle of mourners, a woman who would remove her veil and reveal herself to be my mother, her eyes moistening in regret, and this would bring me closer to believing in God. It provided me with an incentive; it provided me with compassion.

Someone asked me to look up at a camera. I raised my head and obliged.

My mother was strange. She had her reasons. She abandoned her own child. She gave herself to God like a drowning man offering himself to the sea.

She gave herself to emptiness.

She gave herself to pavement.

But she might well live forever, because there would always be men on this earth who needed their hearts inflamed, men with not a sliver of my father's determination or charm who would like to think they could turn her around. To them, she would remain a sympathetic voice.

They hissed at my father.

Above, in the distance, I could see a dark cloud.

The coffin was wheeled from the antechamber to the church, in front of the altar. The church was modest and somber, unlike yesterday's chapel with its salmon-pink carpet and soft light. It was cramped and stark, its whitewashed walls interrupted by stained-glass windows and a lonely bronze crucifix behind the altar. It smelled of incense, layers of incense old and new, the scent encrusted in the pews and the coffee-colored carpet. The place seemed almost greasy from it. Another priest, not Father Felix, but an older man with a dark face and droopy eyes, conducted the Mass. He led us through the Our Father again. He read from the New Testament. I'd forgotten how participatory Masses could be. We stood up and sat down, we made the sign of the cross, we responded, "Blessed be the Lord." A Mass—heavy, crowded, victimized by gravity. We offered peace to the people seated beside us. I shook my own father's hand halfheartedly and said, "Peace be with you." He mumbled it back to me with menace. The old priest offered Communion to those who belonged to the Church, and blessings to everyone else. We, the bereaved family—my father and I, then Jana—were first in line. The priest placed the back of his hand against my cheek, his hound-dog eyes set on my face in sympathy, and, though I was never confirmed, placed a Communion wafer on my tongue. It felt dry in my mouth and left no taste as I swallowed.

The graveyard was near full occupancy, I figured. Her grave was at a far corner, away from the chapel and the shade of the older sections with their prim balsams and leafy birches. The plot next to hers was newly filled: soggy wreaths of white daisies still stood huddled crookedly around it. The coffin was lowered by straps into the ground, as more ridiculous hymns were sung and people behind us let out muffled sobs.

My father stood beside me, before the open rectangular hole in the ground, perfectly silent. He hadn't said a word in the car to the cemetery. He looked in pain. Maybe because of an ulcer he'd picked up when he first moved to Toronto, which returned during times of stress, or because of the music business and his friends here still in it who remembered the humiliating incident with his first wife, which led to his own early retirement from stardom. Maybe because of the funeral and the money that kept slipping away from him, previously spent by his second wife and his son, someone who utterly lacked any appreciation for him. But then again, he always looked in pain. That was the way fathers looked, like shrapnel was being wrenched from their stomachs, like needles had been slid under their fingernails.

The canopy that had been set up over the grave cast a shadow on his face. He kept calm, even as a small crane began hoisting dirt into the hole. We watched the hole fill; then the operator used the rear of the machine to pack the dirt into the ground. My mother was being buried, noisily.

The dark cloud in the distance grew.

And then, without warning, my father's eyes flung open and he cried out, surprised, a high-pitched yelp that drew everyone's attention.

I recognized her. It was the woman from the doughnut shop. Anders's love object, the reason for his strange threats. She was also the woman who had performed "Bushmills" at karaoke night. She had jumped a fence and dodged the policeman running after her. Now she was on my father's back, her press-on fingernails ripping into his face. She was in high heels, this heavyset woman with square jaw and thick arms, a black veil covering her face. There was a bulge in the belt cinching her suit jacket that glinted in the light—it was a gun. Gord and Father Felix rushed forward and pulled the woman off. Dad, still howling, spun around and tripped on his own feet, and fell to the ground.

"Like the dog you are!" she yelled. "Like the dog you are!"

With her arm extended and shaking, she assumed a combat stance, lifted the revolver, and pointed it at my father. Even though this happened quickly, I watched my father's face as I had all day. On it was an expression of serenity. The woman's face was fat and pink with what seemed like gleeful blood lust. Then this apparent confidence was replaced by a look of confusion and panic—two or three darting glances, a twitch. She swung the gun to her head, set its shiny silver barrel up to her temple, and fired. As she toppled over, her veil came off, her wig came off. This woman was a man. She was another man who loved my mother.

Dad lay sprawled on the ground above my mother's grave, rubbing his eyes, his face set in a baby's grimace. I could see the back of his mouth. I held out my hand to him. Tears were running down his face as he took it.

I managed to finish high school, after all. Jana rejoiced. This, in spite of the suspension Navi and I were given for the balance of the school year. We took the fall, not for the infamous walkout, which caused no damage, or the toxic nerve gas scare, which we had nothing to do with, but for vandalism, after a man at the hardware store called to report our suspicious behavior with spray paints. Navi's folks were royally pissed off, naturally, even though there was no need to worry. He had already received his acceptance letters and full scholarships from three different universities. Mr. Choi, the principal, brought our parents in and made it sound as if he were doing us a gigantic favor by not expelling us, by allowing us to graduate. We were to go to school for our provincials, but to stay away otherwise. So we ended up studying together at the public library. Navi helped me catch up on a year's worth of English, chemistry, and math. I wasn't a bad student after all, not if I sucked it up and did the work.

I attended my graduation ceremony, where I saw Rose for the first time in weeks. She looked happy. I realized I'd never seen her that way, so free of whatever had been bothering her, and it felt as though she was done with me. She seemed to float around in her tacky gabardine graduation gown. I lost track of her on the auditorium stage, but after the last speech was given, she tapped me on the shoulder. She smiled and shook my hand and said she was glad to see me, when it was obvious to me she wasn't. Rose had a face incapable of deception. "You look good," I said in a hopeless attempt at flattery.

"I'm fine with how I look," she replied, a little coldly.

She smiled again, this time without looking into my eyes, then returned to her parents.

Both Jana and my father attended my graduation. Jana took pictures of us in which we all looked happy, almost lighthearted. We went out for dinner with Gord and pregnant Nadine, and at the restaurant Dad opened a briefcase full of twenty-dollar bills and passed it across the table. My graduation present. Trust Dad to part so dramatically with his cash. Ten thousand dollars.

"It's up to you what you do with it," he said.

Jana put her hand on mine and nodded. They were attending weekly counseling sessions.

In August, I took a train across the country, the same trip my mother had made thirty years earlier. I wanted to get to the Maritimes, but after four days without sleep in my second-class seat, I found myself in Toronto. I looked up Nathan Shaw and stayed with him and his wife. Maybe it was the old family charisma, but Mrs. Shaw took to me and said I could stay as long as I wanted. I liked her. She was thin, taller than Nathan, with long spindly fingers, dusty-blond hair, and an almost English lilt at the end of her questions that made her sound delicate, maybe brittle. That night, we had something with pheasant and mint for dinner and then retired to the attic porch, where we sipped wine from a bottle that rested on the window ledge next to an air conditioner. This was what my parents had missed out on: it wasn't too bad.

I told Mrs. Shaw I'd never eaten as well at someone's home. She was slumped in a wicker chair, out of which, I would learn later in my stay, it was nearly impossible to move.

"We eat in all the time," she said, pointing a leftover bread-stick at Nathan, "because he doesn't like lineups. He has panic attacks unless we sit by the window. I would say he has a functional fear of crowds."

"I would say 'functional' is a convenient word, isn't it?" he responded.

Mrs. Shaw smirked, and shot me a sidelong look.

"A funny man, he is. That's why we keep him around."

"I like to think that I'm only being fire-conscious," Nathan continued, "more prescient in the arena of disaster. I know a thing or two about human nature. I was, after all, a child of the sixties."

Mrs. Shaw burst out laughing.

She said she was glad to have me here. Both their children, aged twenty-one and nineteen, lived away from home during the school year and were in Europe this summer. They were sisters who got along so poorly that each phoned home every few days to learn the whereabouts of the other, to avoid being in the same country.

I was glad to accept the Shaws' hospitality. I told them I wanted to spend a week in Toronto, but I ended up staying more than a month. For the first few days, I hung around the house, eating all their peanut butter and Premium Plus crackers, excited about the different TV stations in Ontario. Nathan and I bummed around occasionally. We went to Italian bakeries and watched women on the street, but even though he was funny and sarcastic, it was still like hanging around someone's parent.

"Have you read my book?" he asked me point-blank one afternoon while we were watching televised rugby.

I nodded. I was about to say something about it, the thing I had prepared to say about it, but he interrupted me.

"I guess I haven't talked much about Helena. It's not as though I've been afraid. It's more as though I don't know where to begin." His face sort of screwed up, an almost oxygen-deficient expression, and he mumbled. "How's this—I'll write it down."

"Good for you," I said, punching him in the arm. "I'll be in the kitchen if you need any moral support."

I considered calling people I knew in the city. I thought about ringing Leslie Erickson, the man who wrote my parents' biography, the weirdo who had spent all of June pestering me about my life story. But I decided to go to the Hockey Hall of Fame instead, where I stared at the memorabilia—international jerseys and historic sticks. The Stanley Cup was out for the summer, but I saw the other trophies and watched videotaped replays of vicious slashes. The entrance to the Hall was, like a lot of Toronto, part of an underground mall. It led to a food court, where I had a piece of gourmet Thai pizza.

From there I stared at my map and figured out how to get to Yorkville, the neighborhood once composed of narrow, Victorian row houses. Back in 1967, there was a riot and hippies blocked off the streets for three days after police broke up a downtown Happening. The hippies wanted the street closed to traffic, and the city wanted the area cleaned up and turned into a shopping center. It looked as though the city had won. The brick houses of Yorkville were now upscale boutiques and restaurants. Places like the Riverboat and the Village Corner became obsolete in the seventies, after the drinking age was dropped to eighteen. I walked along Bloor Street and tried to imagine my parents here, my dad in his very own army-surplus jacket, ringlets of blond hair covering his face, running into my mother, wispy and quiet, disconcertingly seductive under her soft words. I sat on a bench a block from the subway station, facing the weeds and rubble of an empty lot, and then, at its far end, the front façade of an otherwise demolished building. It looked ancient and ruined. I wanted to talk to the walls, to share my story with them.

Whenever I called home, Jana would inevitably answer the phone, picking up after the first ring, eager to hear from me.

"Did you hear about the man they arrested for making the threats?" she asked once. "He had an entire shack, an abandoned barn, where he made real toxic nerve gas. The walls of the shack were covered with pornography."

"Tell me how you are."

"We're doing well," she said. "I've been helping Nadine with her knitting for the baby. She's been poking herself a lot."

I asked about my father, who had been depressed after the funeral. He puttered around with his guitar in the new kitchen, filled with nervous energy, electing not to eat or drink. For once we wanted him to get nice and drunk and let it all out, but he had stopped drinking in the same effortless way he had given up smoking. We watched him shrivel in his newfound sobriety, his clothes falling loosely. Jana pleaded for him to get help, which he did only out of vanity once his hair started falling out in clumps.

"Why don't you have a word with him," Jana suggested. I hesitated, and to fill the silence, she whispered, "He's responded well to the medication."

I heard my father asking to talk, then Jana passing the phone over to him.

"I'm on something," he said, his voice dripping with cheer. "Though being on it makes me forget what it is."

"How are you?"

"I'm surviving, Saul. I talk to a man with a funny Austrian accent. We've decided that I'm the gloomiest songwriter of my generation. The word he uses is *Lebensmüde*."

"Good."

"Are you having a good time?"

"I am."

There was a pause, as though he had reconsidered saying what he was about to say. "When are you coming back?"

"Before Christmas, I think." I planned to be home for Christmas. Then I would figure out where to go next.

"Excellent. Come back safely. You'll get to meet Dr. Blum at the group session. He happens to be a fan."

I went to a lake an hour from Toronto. I set up a borrowed tent in a clearing off the beach and sat on a log that day. The water was silver and clear. Was this where my grandfather used to take me? I couldn't remember. Maybe. It was nearly impossible to see the other end. I got back to town and met up with Navi, who was starting his degree at York University. I left Toronto and spent a week in Montreal, where I met a bunch of Australian kids my age, bumming around like me. I was like any other carefree kid traveling around on someone else's dime. I decided to be that kid—a reasonable facsimile, at the very least—full of drunken goodwill, optimistic and cash-rich, ready to screw if the opportunity arose. I tried very hard to be him.

I visited Marina and Louise in New York, where I toured museums by myself during the day and played crazy eights with them at night. Louise was back at school while attempting to sell her screenplay. She said that she was busy stalking Loudon Wainwright III, and laughed. Then she kissed the cover of his 1975 album, *Unrequited*, which featured a big picture of Wainwright, bearded and long-faced, with a glycerin tear running down his cheek.

Marina was working at the mattress warehouse and taking Yiddish lessons. She had dyed her hair black. She was kind enough not to say anything, but I got the sense she was in love with someone. I just knew it. Still, we got along merrily and I slept on their living room futon alone.

I spent another week in Boston and made my way slowly west, renting a car in Providence and following signs until I bought a road atlas somewhere in Ohio. I spent four days in Las Vegas, drinking cheap Corona with off-duty kitchen staff at Circus Circus, before going to see Bryce Canyon. I met a woman there, a bartender named Tina whom I nearly slept with, but she kicked me out of her apartment when I made fun of her taste in movies. I drove down to Arizona and spent a night in the desert, off an abandoned road. The stars above were pristine, scrubbed of smog and far away from city lights. And the only sounds were of free-range cattle mooing in the distance. I dreamt about how nice it would be to sleep in my own bed. I thought about going home and in a few months holding Gord and Nadine's kid, little Helena, and let my eyes close. I dreamt about cooing at little babies, winning their hearts over with my charismatic cooing, as I slept in my rental, a brown Toyota Celica. It had only a radio, so I would listen to AM stations, mostly talk and religious programming, interrupted by an occasional Everly Brothers tune. I searched along the dial for my parents' songs, and only once did I hear them, around sunset, just outside Ogden, Utah. It was late November and I had been in the car for hours, long enough not to notice the gorgeous rock formations, slabs of flat mesa, square and craggy and the color of sunburnt flesh. The sky ahead seemed to press the horizon low to the ground and loomed heavy with clouds, sheets of clouds that grew gray in the distance. Off the road were desert scrub and Day-Glo road signs. Then I saw a field of tree stumps, jagged and dark in yellow grass, that sort of resembled a flock of petrified sheep. I had been switching radio stations compulsively, this after drinking cups and cups of coffee. The coffee gave me panic attacks, and I drove with geriatric caution as thoughts of mangled sedans and human splatter crossed my mind. I slowed the car down, drifting toward the gravelly shoulder as I turned the dial. I felt my mother's voice, felt it along the back of my neck, felt my heart pounding from caffeine, and for the first time in my life, I longed to be home. I drove toward the moon rising in the pale light of dusk.

ACKNOWLEDGMENTS

First, I'd like to offer thanks to my teachers: Michael Cunning-ham, Eduardo Machado, Fenton Johnson, Helen Schulman, David Plante.

The following people were indispensable, as readers and friends, while I was writing the novel: Marika Alzadon, Margret Bollerup, Christina Chiu, Mark Constantinescu, Sara Frank, Darren Hayward, Dave King, Alec Michod, Derek Mitchell, Ken Orchard, Larry Sacks, Geoff Thompson.

As for the publication process, I would like to thank my editor, Barbara Berson; my agent, Beverley Slopen; my brother Danny and my friends Lee Henderson and Steve Galloway for their encouragement, counsel, and formidable lunching abilities. Extra thanks to Aimee Taub at Putnam for having faith in this, and to Anna Jardine for her copyediting brilliance.

While writing this novel, I consulted the following books for information about Canadian music and culture in the 1960s: John Einarson, *Neil Young: Don't Be Denied: "The Canadian Years"* (Kingston, Ontario: Quarry Press, 1992); Nicholas Jennings, *Before the Gold Rush: Flashbacks to the Dawn of the Canadian Sound* (Toronto: Viking, 1997); Margaret Trudeau, *Beyond Reason* (New York: Paddington Press, 1979). The German phrases quoted in the book were found on the "Dirty Crap to Say in German" website (www.eat-germany.net/crap/dirtcrap.htm).

A few more notes: "Baroque-a-Nova" is the title of a song by Mason Williams that was once found on the jukebox at Helen's Grill (Main and Twenty-fifth) in Vancouver. The unnamed town where the novel is set is based *loosely* on Ladner, a suburb of Vancouver where I lived from ages five to twelve, and one I remember fondly, if not completely accurately.

Kevin Chong was born in Hong Kong in 1975 and moved with his family to Vancouver in 1977. He spent his formative years noodling on the guitar, playing in garage punk bands, and listening to a lot of Neil Young. He graduated from the University of British Columbia in 1997 and earned his MFA in creative writing at Columbia University three years later. Chong lives in Vancouver, where he is at work on a second novel.